THE PRINCE OF MIST

THE PRINCE OF MIST

CARLOS RUIZ ZAFÓN

TRANSLATED BY
LUCIA GRAVES

LB

LITTLE, BROWN AND COMPANY
New York · Boston

Little, Brown and Company

Hachette Book Group
237 Park Avenue, New York, NY 10017
Visit our website at www.lb-teens.com

Little, Brown and Company is a division of Hachette Book Group, Inc.
The Little, Brown name and logo are trademarks of Hachette Book Group, Inc.

The publisher is not responsible for websites (or their content)
that are not owned by the publisher.

First U.S. Trade Paperback Edition: April 2011
First U.S. Hardcover Edition: May 2010
First Little, Brown and Company International Edition: May 2010

Library of Congress Cataloging-in-Publication Data

Ruiz Zafón, Carlos, 1964–
[El Príncipe de la Niebla. English]
The Prince of Mist / by Carlos Ruiz Zafón ; translated by Lucia Graves.—1st ed.
p. cm.
Summary: In 1943, in a seaside town where their family has gone to be safe from war,
thirteen-year-old Max Carver and his sister, fifteen-year-old Alicia, with their new friend
Roland, face off against an evil magician who is striving to complete a bargain made
before he died.
ISBN 978-0-316-04477-6 (hc) / 978-0-316-04480-6 (pb)
[1. Supernatural—Fiction. 2. Magic—Fiction. 3. Dead—Fiction. 4. Brothers and
sisters—Fiction. 5. Shipwrecks—Fiction. 6. Family life—Europe—Fiction. 7. Europe—
History—1918–1945—Fiction.] I. Graves, Lucia. II. Title.
PZ7.R8868Pri 2010   [Fic]—dc22   2009051256

10 9 8 7 6 5 4 3 2 1

RRD-C
Printed in the United States of America

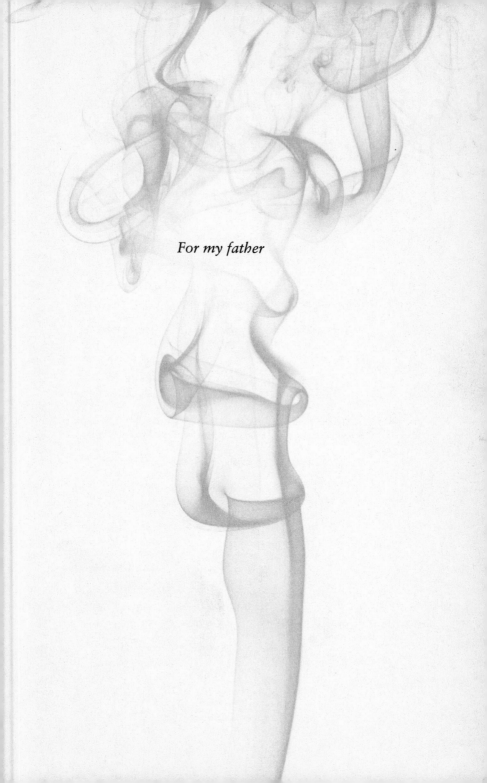

For my father

A NOTE FROM THE AUTHOR

Dear Reader,

The Prince of Mist is the first novel I ever published, and it marked the beginning of my career as a writer in 1992. Readers familiar with my later work, such as *The Shadow of the Wind* or *The Angel's Game*, may not know that my first four novels were originally published as young adult books. Although they are mainly aimed at young readers, my hope was that they would appeal to readers of all ages. In creating those books, I tried to write the kind of novels that I would have liked to read as a kid, but that also would continue to interest me at the age of twenty-three, or forty, or eighty-three.

For years the rights to these books were "trapped" in a legal dispute but now can finally be enjoyed by readers around the world. Since their original publication, these earlier works of mine have fortunately been well received by those who are young, and those who are not so young. I like to believe that storytelling transcends age limitations, and I hope readers of my adult novels will be tempted to explore these stories of magic, mystery, and adventure. Lastly, to all new readers, I hope you will come to enjoy these novels too as you begin your own adventures inside the world of books.

Safe travels,
CARLOS RUIZ ZAFÓN
MAY 2010

1

MAX WOULD NEVER FORGET that faraway summer when, almost by chance, he discovered magic. It was 1943, and the winds of war were dragging the world relentlessly toward the abyss. In the middle of June, on Max's thirteenth birthday, his father, an eccentric watch-maker and inventor of dazzling if completely imprac-tical devices, gathered the family in the living room to announce that this would be their last day in the lofty apartment perched high above the oldest part of the city, a place that had been their home ever since Max could remember. A deathly silence fell upon the members of the Carver family. They looked at each other, and then at the watchmaker. He had that smile on his face they all knew so well, the one that always meant he had bad news or another of his crazy ideas.

"We are moving," he announced, "to a beach house in a small town on the coast. We're getting out of this city and away from the war."

Max gulped, then timidly raised his hand in protest. The other members of the family joined in, but the watchmaker waved away their concerns. He was on a roll now, and he laid out his plan with military precision. There would be no going back on the decision: They were leaving the next morning at dawn. Now they had to pack up their most prized possessions and prepare for the long journey to their new home.

In truth, the family was not entirely surprised by the news. They all suspected that the idea of leaving the city in search of a better place to live had been on Maximilian Carver's mind for some time—everyone, that is, except his son, Max. To him, the news felt like a mad steam train hurtling through a china shop. His mind went blank, his mouth sagged, and his eyes glazed over. As he stood, transfixed, it occurred to him that his entire world—his friends at school, everyone he hung out with, even the corner shop where he bought his comics—was about to vanish forever.

While the rest of the family went off to pack up their

belongings, finally resigned to their fate, Max remained staring at his father. The watchmaker knelt down and placed his hands gently on his son's shoulders. The look on Max's face spoke volumes.

"It might seem like the end of the world to you now, Max, but I promise you'll like the place we're moving to. You'll make new friends; you'll see."

"Is it because of the war?" asked Max. "Is that why we have to leave?"

A shadow of sadness fell across his father's eyes. All the drive and conviction of the speech he had made to them earlier was gone, and it occurred to Max that perhaps his father was the one who was most afraid of leaving. But if he had pretended to be excited about the move, then it was because it was the best thing for his family. There was no other option.

"It's bad, isn't it?" Max asked.

"Things'll get better. We'll be back. I promise."

Maximilian Carver hugged his son and smiled mysteriously, then pulled an object out of his jacket pocket and put it in Max's hands. It was a shiny oval that hung from a chain. A pocket watch.

"I made it for you. Happy birthday, Max."

Max opened the silver watch. The hours on the face were marked by moons that waxed and waned to the rhythm of time, and the hands were rays of a sun radiating out from the center of the dial. On the case, engraved in fine script, were the words MAX'S TIME MACHINE.

For a second Max wished his father's latest invention really could stop time. Yet when he raised his eyes and glanced through the window, it already seemed to him as if the light of day was receding and the endless city of spires and domes, of chimneys weaving cobwebs of smoke across the iron skies, had started to fade away.

Years later, as he remembered the scene, his family wandering to and fro with their bags while he sat in a corner clutching the watch his father had given him, Max knew that this was the day he left his childhood behind.

♦ ♦ ♦

That night Max didn't sleep a wink. While the rest of the family slept, he lay awake, dreading the dawn when he would have to say good-bye to the small universe he had built for himself over the years. The hours crept by silently as he lay stretched out on his bed, his eyes lost in the blue shadows that danced on the ceiling, as if he might find in them some oracle that could predict his destiny; in his hand was the watch his father had made for him. The moons glowed in the darkness of the night— perhaps they held the answer to all the questions he had begun to ask himself that afternoon.

Finally, day began to break over the horizon in a streak of red light. Max jumped out of bed and went down to the living room. His father was sitting in an armchair, fully dressed, reading a book by the light of an oil lamp. Max was not the only one who had spent a sleepless night. The watchmaker smiled at him and closed his book.

"What are you reading?" asked Max, pointing at the thick volume.

"It's a book about Copernicus. I take it you know who he is?" asked Mr. Carver.

"I do go to school, you know," said Max.

His father sometimes still treated him as if he were a child.

"Well, what do you know about him?" his father asked insistently.

"He discovered that the earth turns around the sun, not the other way around."

"Not bad. And do you know what that means?"

"Problems," Max replied.

The watchmaker smiled and handed Max the hefty tome.

"Here, it's yours. Read it."

Max inspected the mysterious leather-bound volume. It looked as if it was a thousand years old and might house the spirit of some age-old genie trapped in its pages by an ancient curse.

"Well, now," his father said abruptly, "who's going to wake your sisters?"

Without looking up from the book, Max shook his head to indicate that he was granting his father the honor of dragging his two sisters—Alicia, aged fifteen, and Irina, aged eight—out of their beds.

While Maximilian Carver walked off to give the rest of the family their wake-up call, Max settled into the armchair and began to read. He lost himself in the words and images conjured in his mind, and for a while he forgot that his family was going anywhere. He found himself flying among stars and planets, but then he looked up and saw his mother standing next to him with tears in her eyes.

"You and your sisters were born in this house," she murmured.

"We'll be back," he said, echoing his father's words. "You'll see."

His mother smiled at him and kissed him on the forehead.

"As long as you're with me, I don't care where we go," she said.

His mother had a way of reading his thoughts. Half an hour later, the entire family crossed the front doorway for the last time, heading toward a new life. Summer had begun.

♦ ♦ ♦

Max had once read in one of his father's books that some childhood images become engraved in the mind like photographs, like scenes you can return to again and again and will always remember, no matter how much time goes by. He understood the meaning of those words the first time he saw the sea. The family had been traveling on the train for over three hours when, all of a sudden, they emerged from a dark tunnel and Max found himself gazing at an endless expanse of ethereal light, the electric blue of the sea shimmering beneath the midday sun, imprinting itself on his retina like a supernatural apparition. The ashen light that perpetually drowned the old city already seemed like a distant memory. He felt as if he had spent his entire life looking at the world through a black-and-white lens and suddenly it had sprung into life in full, luminous color he could almost touch. As the train continued its journey only a few meters from the shore, Max leaned out the window and, for the first time ever, felt the touch of salty wind on his skin. He turned to look at his father, who was watching him from the other end of the compartment with his mysterious smile, nodding in reply to a question Max hadn't even asked. At that moment, Max promised himself that whatever their destination, whatever the name of the station this train was taking them to, from that day on he would never live anywhere where he couldn't wake up every morning to see that same dazzling blue light that rose toward heaven like some magical essence.

♦ ♦ ♦

While Max stood on the platform watching the train ride away through clouds of steam, Mr. Carver left his family standing beside their suitcases outside the stationmaster's office and went off to negotiate a reasonable price for the transportation of luggage, people, and paraphernalia to their final destination. Max's first impression of the town, judging from the station and the few houses he could see, their roofs peeping timidly over the surrounding trees, was that it looked like one of those miniature villages, the sort you got with train sets, where the imaginary inhabitants were in danger of falling off a table if they wandered too far. Max was busy contemplating this variation on Copernicus's theory of the universe when his mother's voice rescued him from his daydream.

"Well, Max. What's the verdict?"

"It's too soon to tell," he answered. "It looks like a model, like those ones you see in toy-shop windows."

"Maybe it is," his mother said, smiling. "But don't tell your father," she went on. "Here he comes now."

Maximilian Carver was escorted by two burly porters

whose clothes were splattered with grease stains, soot, and other unidentifiable substances. Both had thick mustaches and wore sailor's caps as if this was their uniform.

"This is Robin and Philip," the watchmaker explained. "Robin will take the luggage and Philip will take us. Is that all right?"

Max wasn't clear who was Philip and who was Robin, and he wondered if they could even tell themselves, but he chose to keep his mouth shut. Without waiting for the family's approval, the two men walked over to the mountain of trunks, and each hoisted up the largest ones as if they weighed nothing. Max pulled out his watch and looked at the face with its curving moons. It was two o'clock. The old station clock said half past twelve.

"The station clock is slow," muttered Max.

"You see?" his father replied excitedly. "We've only just arrived and already there's work here for us."

His mother gave a faint smile, as she always did when Maximilian Carver had one of his bursts of radiant optimism, but Max could see a hint of sadness in her eyes, that peculiar light that, ever since he was a child, had led him to believe that his mother could foresee events in the future that the rest of them could not even dream of.

"Everything's going to be all right, Mum," he said, feeling like an idiot the moment he'd spoken.

His mother stroked his cheek.

"Of course, Max. Everything's going to be fine."

Suddenly, Max felt certain that someone was looking at him. He spun around and saw a large cat staring at him through the bars of one of the station windows. The cat blinked and, with a prodigiously agile leap for an animal of that size, jumped through the window, padded over to Irina, and rubbed its back against her pale ankles, meowing softly. Max's sister knelt down to stroke it, then picked it up in her arms. The cat let itself be cuddled and gently licked the little girl's fingers. Irina smiled, spellbound, and, still cradling the animal in her arms, walked over to where her family was waiting.

"We've only just got here and already you've picked up some disgusting beast. Goodness knows what it's infested with," Alicia snapped.

"It's not a disgusting beast. It's a cat and it's been abandoned," replied Irina. "Mum?"

"Irina, we haven't even got to the house yet."

Irina pulled a face, to which the cat contributed a sweet, seductive meow.

"It can stay in the garden. Please…"

Alicia rolled her eyes. Max watched his older sister. She had not opened her mouth since they had left the city; her expression was impenetrable and her eyes seemed to be lost in the distance. If anyone in the family was not overjoyed by the promise of a new life it was Alicia. Max

10

was tempted to make a joke about "Her Highness the Ice Princess," but decided not to. Something told him that his sister had left behind much more in the city than he could possibly imagine.

"It's fat and it's ugly," Alicia added. "Are you really going to let her get her own way again?"

Irina threw a steely glare at her older sister, an open declaration of war unless the latter kept her mouth shut. Alicia held her gaze for a few moments and then turned around, sighing with frustration, and walked over to where the porters were loading the luggage. On the way she passed her father, who noticed her red face.

"Quarreling already?" asked Maximilian Carver. "What's the matter?"

Irina presented the cat to her father. The feline, to its credit, purred adoringly. Never one to falter in the face of authority, Irina proceeded to make her case with a determination she had inherited from her father.

"It's all alone in the world. Someone's abandoned it. We can't leave it here. Can we take it with us? It can live in the garden and I'll look after it. I promise," Irina said, her words spilling over each other.

The watchmaker looked in astonishment at the cat, then at his wife.

"You always said caring for an animal gives a person a sense of responsibility," Irina added.

"Did I ever say that?"

"Many times. Those exact words."

Her father sighed.

"I don't know what your mother will say...."

"And what do *you* say, Maximilian Carver?" asked Mrs. Carver, with a grin that showed her amusement at what had now become her husband's dilemma.

"Well...we'd have to take it to the vet and..."

"Pleeease..." whimpered Irina.

The watchmaker and his wife exchanged a look.

"Why not?" concluded Maximilian Carver, who could not bear the thought of starting the summer with a family feud. "But you'll have to look after it. Promise?"

Irina's face lit up. The cat's pupils narrowed to a slit until they looked like black needles against the luminous gold of its eyes.

"Come on! Hurry up!" said the watchmaker. "The luggage has been loaded."

Holding the cat in her arms, Irina ran toward the van. The creature, its head leaning on the girl's shoulder, kept its eyes nailed on Max defiantly.

"It was waiting for us," he muttered to himself.

"Don't just stand there in a daze, Max. Move it," his father insisted as he walked over to the van, hand in hand with his wife.

Max followed, reluctantly.

Just then, something made him turn around and look again at the blackened face of the ancient station clock. He examined it carefully. Something about it didn't add up. Max remembered perfectly well that when they reached the station the clock had said half past midday. Now, the hands pointed at ten minutes to twelve.

"Max!" his father called from the van. "We're leaving!"

"Coming," Max said to himself, his eyes still riveted to the clock.

The clock was not slow; it worked perfectly but with one peculiarity: It went backward.

2

THE CARVERS' NEW HOME STOOD at the end of a long beach that stretched along the sea; the blanket of white sand was dotted here and there with small islands of wild grass that rippled in the wind. The town itself, from which the beach extended, was made up of ornate Victorian houses arranged in a long, winding parade of spiky gables and colorful sash windows. Most were painted a soft pastel color, their gardens and white fences all neatly aligned, reinforcing Max's first impression that the place looked like a collection of dollhouses. On their way, they drove through the town, along the main street and past the town square, while Maximilian Carver filled them in about the enchantments of their new home with the enthusiasm of a tour guide.

It seemed a peaceful place, wrapped in the same luminosity that had captivated Max when he saw the ocean for the first time. Judging from what he could see, most of the town's inhabitants favored bicycles to get about or simply walked. The streets were spotlessly clean and the only sound, except for the occasional rumble of a motor, was the soft pounding of the sea on the beach. As they passed through, Max noticed his family's different reactions to what was going to be the new landscape of their lives. Irina and her feline ally gazed at the neat rows of streets and houses with a calm curiosity, as if they already felt at home. Alicia, predictably, seemed a thousand miles away, lost in her thoughts, confirming Max's conviction that he knew little or nothing about his older sister. Teenage girls, thought Max, were a mystery of evolution not even Copernicus himself could fathom.

His mother regarded the village with resignation, maintaining a forced smile to disguise the anxiety that, for some reason Max could not decipher, had taken hold of her. Finally, Maximilian Carver observed his new habitat triumphantly, glancing at each member of his clan who, in turn, responded with an approving smile—anything else might have broken the watchmaker's heart, so convinced was he that he had led his family to a new paradise.

As Max surveyed the tranquil streets bathed in warm sunlight, the specter of war seemed very far away, almost unreal. Perhaps, he thought, his father's decision to move to this place was an inspired one. By the time the van was heading up the road leading to their beach house, Max had already forgotten about the station clock and the jitters that Irina's new friend had produced in him. Scanning the horizon, he thought he could distinguish the black silhouette of a ship sailing like a mirage through the haze that rose from the ocean's surface. Seconds later, it had disappeared.

◆ ◆ ◆

Their new home was spread over two floors, stood some fifty meters from the edge of the beach, and was surrounded by a garden with a white fence that was badly in need of a fresh coat of paint. The house itself was built of wood and, with the exception of its dark roof, was also painted white and seemed to be in a reasonably good state, considering its proximity to the sea and the wear and tear the damp, salty wind must have inflicted on it.

As they drove toward the house, Maximilian Carver told his family that it had been built in 1924 for a prestigious surgeon from the city, Dr. Richard Fleischmann, and his wife, Eva, to serve as their seaside home during the summer months. At the time, the whole project had seemed a bit strange to the local population. The Fleischmanns were a solitary couple with no children and mostly kept to themselves. Despite this, and because nothing much ever happened in the town, the local gossips latched on to this information and quickly reached a consensus that the couple was probably trying to leave something behind. Bad memories, most likely. The kind that follow you no matter how far you go. On his first visit, Dr. Fleischmann had made it clear that the builders and all the building materials were to come directly from the city. Such a whim practically tripled the cost of the house, but the surgeon seemed to have plenty of money to pay for such an expense. *City folk,* the locals thought, *they think money can buy everything.*

Throughout the winter of 1923, the locals eyed the endless coming and going of workers and trucks with mild suspicion, while day by day the skeleton of the house at the end of the beach slowly began to rise. Finally, the following spring, the decorators gave the house one last lick of paint, and a few weeks later the couple moved in for the summer. Whatever bad memories had been trailing them, the house by the beach seemed to be the lucky charm that changed the Fleischmanns' fortunes. The surgeon's wife, who, again according to confidential information shared only by the local gossips, had been unable to conceive a child as a result of an accident she'd suffered some years earlier, became pregnant that first year. And on June 23, 1925, assisted by her husband, she gave birth to a son, whom they named Jacob.

The local legend was that little Jacob was a blessing from heaven and his arrival transformed the bitter, solitary nature of the Fleischmanns. Soon the doctor and his wife began to make friends among the townspeople, and they became popular with their neighbors during the happy years they spent in their house by the sea. That is, until the tragedy of 1932. In June of that year, early one morning, Jacob drowned while playing on the beach near his home.

All the joy the couple had discovered through their beloved son was gone forever. During the winter of 1932, Dr. Fleischmann's health deteriorated, and soon his doctors knew he would not live to see the next summer. A year later, the widow's lawyers put the house up for sale. It remained empty and without a buyer, forgotten at the end of the beach.

This was how, quite by chance, Maximilian Carver had come to hear of its existence. The watchmaker was on his way back from a trip to buy equipment and tools for his workshop when he spent the night in the town. While he was dining in the small local hotel he struck up a conversation with the owner and told him that he'd always longed to live in a small town like that one. The hotel owner told him about the house, and Maximilian decided to delay his return so that he could have a look at it the following day. On the way back to the city, he chewed over figures and the possibility of opening a watchmaker's shop in the town. It took him eight months to announce the move to his family, but at the bottom of his heart he had made up his mind the moment he saw the house by the beach.

◆ ◆ ◆

In time, the memories of that first day would come back to Max as a peculiar collection of random images. To begin with, as soon as the van stopped outside the house and Robin and Philip had started to unload the luggage, Mr. Carver managed to trip over an old bucket, propelling himself at dizzying speed onto the white fence and knocking down at least four meters of it.

"Are you all right, dear?" asked his wife.

"Never better," he replied, his right foot still trapped in the bucket. "It's a sign of good luck."

"I knew he was going to say that," muttered Alicia.

Mrs. Carver shot her a warning look.

The two porters carried the luggage as far as the front porch and, apparently considering their mission accomplished, vanished in an instant, leaving the family to do the honors of dragging the trunks up the stairs.

"Another good omen," Alicia commented drily.

When Maximilian Carver solemnly opened the front door, a musty smell wafted out through the opening like a ghost that had been trapped between the walls for many years. Inside, a thin haze of dust hovered in the faint light that filtered through the blinds in slanting razors of gold.

"My God," Max's mother muttered to herself as she estimated the tons of dust that would have to be removed.

"Isn't it marvelous?" Maximilian Carver asked hurriedly. "I told you so."

Max exchanged a look with Alicia, while Irina gazed openmouthed at the interior of the house. Before anyone could utter another word, Irina's cat jumped out of her arms and charged inside with a loud meow.

"At least somebody likes it," Max heard Alicia grumble.

A second later, following the cat's example, Maximilian Carver stepped into the family's new home.

The first thing Mrs. Carver instructed them to do was open all the doors and windows to air the house. When that had been done, the whole family spent a few hours making the new home habitable. With the precision of a specialized task force, each member attacked a specific job. Alicia was in charge of bedrooms and beds. Irina, duster in hand, knocked down castles of dust, and Max, following her trail, was in charge of sweeping them up. Their mother busied herself distributing the suitcases and made a mental note of all the work that would have to be done. Mr. Carver devoted all his efforts to ensuring that water pipes, electricity, and various mechanical devices were back in working order after years of neglect—which did not turn out to be an easy undertaking.

At last, the whole family gathered on the porch and sat on the steps of their new home for a well-deserved rest, gazing at the silvery hue that was settling over the sea as the afternoon came to an end.

"That's enough for one day," Maximilian Carver said. He was covered in soot and other mysterious residues.

"It will take us a couple of weeks to get the house in shape," Mrs. Carver added. "At the very least."

"There are spiders upstairs," Alicia said. "They're enormous."

"Spiders? Wow!" cried Irina. "What did they look like?"

"They looked just like you," replied Alicia.

"Let's have a peaceful evening, please," their mother interrupted, rubbing the bridge of her nose. "Don't worry about the spiders, Alicia. Max will kill them."

"There's no need to kill them; they can be collected

and put outside in the garden," said the watchmaker. "They're nature's creatures and deserve their day in the sun like the rest of us."

"I always end up with the heroic missions," murmured Max. "Can the extermination — I mean, relocation — wait until tomorrow?"

"Alicia?" their mother pleaded.

"I'm not sleeping in a room full of spiders and goodness knows what else," Alicia declared. "No matter how deserving they are."

"Oh, you're such a princess," said Irina.

"And you're such a brat," replied Alicia.

"Max, before this escalates into a war, will you get rid of the damned spiders?" asked Maximilian Carver in a tired voice.

"So, shall I kill them, or just threaten them a little? I could twist their legs and hand them an eviction notice...." suggested Max.

"Don't start," his mother cut in.

"Do as your mother says," his father warned.

Max stood and gave a military salute, then went inside the house, ready to wipe out its previous lodgers by all means possible. As he climbed the stairs to the upper floor, he saw the glittering eyes of Irina's cat watching him steadily from the top step. It seemed to be guarding the upper floor like a sentinel. He stopped for a second, then resumed his climb. He was not going to be afraid of a stray cat; he would not give it the satisfaction. As soon as Max went into one of the bedrooms, the cat followed him.

◆ ◆ ◆

The wooden flooring creaked softly under his feet. Max began his spider hunt in the rooms facing southwest. From the windows he could see the beach and the sun descending toward the horizon. He examined the floor carefully in search of small, hairy, fast-moving creatures. After the cleaning session, the room was reasonably dirt-free, and it took Max only a couple of minutes to locate the first member of the arachnid family — a fat spider marching from one of the corners in a straight line toward him, as if it were a thuggish ambassador sent on behalf of its species to negotiate a truce. The creature must have been about three centimeters long and had eight black, bristly legs, with a golden mark on its body. No wonder Alicia had panicked. There was no way in the world he was going to pick up that thing and provide it safe passage to the garden. So much for his father's humanistic view of Mother Nature.

Max reached out his hand to grab a broom that was leaning against the wall and got ready to catapult the

23

arachnid into kingdom come. *This is ridiculous,* he thought as he brandished the broom like a deadly weapon. He was steadying himself for the mortal blow when, all of a sudden, Irina's cat pounced on the bug, opened its jaws, and devoured it, chewing vigorously on the spider's body as Max let go of the broom and looked at the cat in astonishment. It threw him a malicious look.

"That's some kitten," he whispered.

The animal swallowed the spider and left the room, presumably in search of its next course. Max walked over to the window. His family was still sitting on the porch. Alicia gave him an inquiring look.

"I wouldn't worry, if I were you, Alicia. I don't think you'll be seeing any more spiders."

"Just make sure," Maximilian Carver insisted.

Max nodded and went to the rooms facing northeast at the back of the house.

He heard the cat prowling nearby and assumed another spider had fallen prey to its lethal claws. The rooms here were smaller than those in the front. Max looked at the view from one of the windows and saw a small backyard with a large garden shed that could be used for storing furniture or as a garage. In the middle of the yard stood a mighty tree, its top reaching high above the attic windows. Max imagined it must be at least two hundred years old.

Beyond the yard, behind the fence that surrounded the house, was a field of wild grass, and about a hundred meters farther on was what looked like a small enclosure bordered by a wall of pale stone. The vegetation had invaded the grounds, transforming the enclosure into a jungle from which emerged what seemed to be figures: human figures. In the twilight, Max had to strain his eyes to make out what he was seeing. It appeared to be an abandoned garden. A garden of statues. Max was hypnotized by the strange vision of the figures trapped in the undergrowth, locked inside a walled garden that reminded him of a village graveyard. A gate of metal bars capped with spearheads and locked with chains secured the entrance. Above the spearheads Max could distinguish a shield with a six-pointed star. In the distance, beyond the enclosure, was a thick forest that seemed to extend for miles.

"Made any discoveries?" His mother's voice dragged him from his reverie. "We were beginning to think the spiders had gotten the better of you."

"Over there, next to the wood, there's a walled garden full of statues." Max pointed toward the stone enclosure, and his mother leaned out of the window.

"I can barely see a thing. It's getting dark. Your father and I are heading into town to get something for dinner, at least enough to keep us going until we can do a proper shop tomorrow. Keep an eye on Irina, will you?"

Max nodded. His mother gave him a peck on the cheek and set off down the stairs. Max peered again at the statues in the walled garden, their outlines slowly fading into the evening mist. The breeze had grown cooler. Max closed the window and went off to finish the spider hunt in the other rooms. Irina met him in the hallway.

"Were they big?" she asked, fascinated.

Max hesitated for a second.

"The spiders, Max. Were they big?"

"As big as my fist," Max replied solemnly.

3

THE FOLLOWING DAY, shortly before sunrise, Max heard
a figure wrapped in the nocturnal haze whispering in his
ear. He jumped up, gasping, his heart racing. He was
alone in his room. The image he had dreamed of, that
dark shape murmuring in the shadows, had vanished. He
stretched out a hand toward the bedside table and turned
on the lamp his father had repaired the day before.

Through the window, he saw dawn breaking over the
forest. A thick mist was moving slowly across the field of
wild grass, but now and then the breeze opened up gaps
through which he could just about make out the silhouettes
of the statues in the walled garden. Max took his pocket

watch from the bedside table and opened it. The smiling moons shone like plates of gold. It was six minutes to six.

Max dressed quietly and crept down the stairs, hoping he wouldn't wake the rest of the family. He went into the kitchen, where the remains of last night's dinner still lay on the wooden table, then opened the door to the backyard and stepped outside. The cold, damp air of early morning nipped at his skin. Making no sound, Max crossed the yard, went through the gate in the fence, closing it behind him, then made his way through the mist toward the walled garden.

♦ ♦ ♦

The path turned out to be longer than he'd expected. From his bedroom window he'd estimated that the walled garden was about a hundred meters from the house, but as he walked through the wild grass Max felt as if he'd covered at least three times that distance when, suddenly, the gate with the spearheads emerged out of the mist.

A rusty chain was fastened around the blackened metal bars, with a corroded old padlock that time had stained a deathly hue. Max pressed his face against the bars and looked inside. The weeds had been gaining ground for years; the enclosure now looked like a neglected greenhouse. Nobody had set foot in that place for ages, thought Max, and whoever the guardian once was, he had long since disappeared.

Max looked around and found a stone the size of his hand next to the garden wall. He picked it up and started pounding at the padlock that linked the two ends of the chain, until at last the old lock snapped open. The chain broke loose, swaying across the bars like a braid of metal hair. Max pushed hard until gradually the two sides of the gate began to give way. When the gap was wide enough for him to get through, Max rested for a moment, then went inside.

The garden was larger than he'd thought. At a glance, he could have sworn there were almost twenty statues half-hidden among the vegetation. He took a few steps forward. The figures seemed to be arranged in concentric circles, and Max realized that they were all facing west. They appeared to form part of something resembling a circus troupe. As he walked among the statues, Max recognized the figure of a lion tamer, a turbaned fakir with a hooked nose, a female contortionist, a strong man, and a whole gallery of other ghostly characters.

In the middle of the garden, resting on a pedestal, stood the imposing figure of a clown. He had one arm outstretched, as if attempting to punch something with his fist, and he wore a glove that was disproportionately large. By the clown's feet, Max noticed a paving stone that seemed to have some kind of design etched on it. He knelt down and pulled back the weeds covering the surface to reveal the outline of a six-pointed star within a circle. Max recognized the symbol: It was identical to the one above the spearheads on the gate.

As he examined the star, Max realized that while at first he had thought the statues were spaced out in concentric rings, they were in fact positioned in a way that mirrored the design of the star, each of the figures standing at an intersection of the lines that formed the shape. Max stood up and gazed at the eerie landscape around him. He looked at the statues in turn, each one swathed in greenery that trembled in the wind, until his eyes rested again on the clown. A shudder ran through his body and he took a step back: The hand of the figure, which seconds earlier had appeared to be clenched in a fist, now lay open, its palm stretched out invitingly. For a moment the cold morning air burned Max's throat, and he could feel a throbbing in his temples.

Slowly, almost fearing he might wake the statues from their eternal sleep, he made his way back to the gate of the enclosure, looking behind him at every step. Once he'd slipped through the gate, he began to run, and this time he didn't look back until he reached the fence guarding the backyard. When he did look, the garden of statues was once again buried in mist.

The smell of buttered toast filled the kitchen. Alicia was staring at her breakfast unenthusiastically, and Irina was pouring milk into a saucer for which the cat didn't display the slightest interest and which it refused to touch. Max observed the scene, suspecting that the cat's eating habits were somewhat unusual and more exotic, as he had discovered the day before. Maximilian Carver held a cup of steaming coffee in his hands and gazed euphorically at his family.

"This morning, I've been conducting some exploratory research in the garden shed," he began, adopting the "here comes the mystery" tone he used when he desperately wanted someone to ask him what he'd discovered.

Max was so familiar with the watchmaker's ways that he sometimes wondered which one of them was the father and which one the son.

"And what have you found?" Max conceded.

"You're not going to believe this," replied his father — although Max thought, *I bet I will*—"a couple of bicycles."

Max raised his eyebrows.

"They're quite old, but with a bit of grease on the chains, they'll go like a bat out of hell," Mr. Carver

31

explained. "And there was something else. I bet you don't know what else I found in the shed?"

"An aardvark," mumbled Irina, still petting her feline friend. Though she was only eight, the youngest of the Carvers had developed a crushing ability for undermining her father's enthusiasm.

"No," replied the watchmaker, visibly annoyed. "Is nobody else going to have a guess?"

Max noticed that his mother had been watching the scene and, realizing that nobody seemed interested in her husband's detective skills, she now came to the rescue.

"A photograph album?" Andrea Carver suggested in her sweetest tone.

"You're getting warmer," replied the watchmaker, feeling encouraged once more. "Max?"

His mother cast him a sidelong glance. Max nodded.

"I don't know. A diary?"

"No. Alicia?"

"I give up," replied Alicia.

"All right, prepare yourselves," said Mr. Carver. "What I've found is a projector. A film projector. And a box full of films."

"What sort of films?" Irina butted in, turning her eyes away from her cat for the first time.

Maximilian Carver shrugged.

"I don't know. Just films. Isn't it fascinating? We can have our own private cinema."

"That's if the projector works," said Alicia.

"Thanks for those words of encouragement, dearest, but let me remind you that your father earns his living mending broken things. The machines and I, we share a secret language."

Andrea Carver placed her hands on her husband's shoulders. "I'm glad to hear that, Mr. Carver," she said, "because someone should be having a serious conversation with the boiler in the basement."

"I'll see to it," replied the watchmaker, standing up and leaving the table.

Alicia followed suit.

"Sit down, miss," said Mrs. Carver quickly. "Breakfast first. You haven't touched it."

"I'm not hungry."

"I'll eat it," volunteered Irina.

Andrea Carver dismissed this proposal.

"She doesn't want to get fat," Irina hissed at her cat, pointing at Alicia.

"I can't eat with that thing waving its tail around the place and shedding hair everywhere," snapped Alicia.

Irina and the creature looked at her with disdain.

"What a princess," Irina grumbled as she went out to the backyard, taking the animal with her.

Alicia turned to her mother, red-faced.

"Why do you always let her do what she wants? When

I was her age you didn't let me get away with half the things she does," Alicia protested.

"Are we going to go over that again?" asked Andrea Carver in a calm voice.

"I wasn't the one who started it," replied her eldest daughter.

"All right. I'm sorry." Andrea Carver gently stroked Alicia's long hair; Alicia tilted her head, avoiding the conciliatory gesture. "But finish your breakfast. Please. Or at least try to start it."

At that moment a metallic bang sounded beneath their feet. They looked at one another.

"Your father in action," their mother commented drily as she downed her coffee. Then she glanced at her son, intrigued.

"You're unusually quiet this morning, Max. Something the matter?"

"Huh?"

Alicia pretended to munch on a piece of toast while Max tried not to think about the extended hand and the bulging eyes of the clown as it grinned through the mist of the walled garden.

4

THE BICYCLES MAXIMILIAN CARVER had rescued from their exile in the garden shed were in much better shape than Max had imagined. He had expected two wiry, rusty skeletons when in fact they looked as if they'd hardly been used. Aided by a couple of dusters and a special liquid for cleaning metal his mother always used, Max discovered that beneath the layers of grime, both bicycles seemed almost new. With his father's help, he greased the chain and the sprockets and pumped up the tires.

"We'll probably have to change the inner tubes at some point," Mr. Carver explained, "but for the time being they'll do."

One of the bicycles was smaller than the other, and as he cleaned them, Max couldn't help thinking about the house's previous owners. He asked himself whether Dr. Fleischmann had bought the bicycles years ago, hoping to go for rides with his son, Jacob, along the beach road. Maximilian Carver saw a shadow of guilt in his son's eyes.

"I'm sure the old doctor would have wanted you to use the bike."

"I'm not so sure," Max muttered. "Why did they leave them here?"

"Sometimes memories follow you wherever you go; you don't need to take them with you," Mr. Carver replied. "I suppose nobody ever used them. Get on. Let's try them out."

Max adjusted the height of his seat and checked the tension of his brake cables.

"We'd better put some more oil on the brakes," Max suggested.

"Just what I thought," the watchmaker agreed, and got down to work. "Listen, Max…"

"Yes, Dad?"

"Don't worry too much about the bikes, okay? What happened to that poor family has nothing to do with us. I probably shouldn't have told you the story," he added, worry clouding his face.

"It's no big deal." Max tightened the brake again. "Now it's perfect."

"Off you go, then."

"Aren't you coming with me?" asked Max.

"I'd love to, but I have to see someone named Fred at ten, in the town. He's going to rent me some space for my shop. Got to think about the business. But if you're still up for it, maybe tomorrow I'll give you a run for your money you'll never forget."

"In your dreams."

"I'm willing to put my money where my mouth is."

"Deal."

Maximilian Carver began gathering up the tools and cleaning his hands with one of the rags. Max watched his father and wondered what he'd been like at his age. People always said that the two of them were alike, but they also said that Irina was like Andrea Carver, a resemblance Max couldn't see even if he tried. It seemed like another of those silly things that whole hordes of unbearable relatives who turned up for Christmas loved to repeat year after year like parrots. Which was a pity, because he wanted it to be true. He wanted to resemble his father.

"Max in one of his trances," Mr. Carver observed with a smile.

"Did you know that there's a walled garden full of

statues behind the house, near the wood?" Max asked, surprising even himself with the question.

"I suppose there are a lot of things around here that we still haven't seen. The garden shed is full of boxes and the basement looks like a museum. If we sold all the junk in this house to an antique dealer, I wouldn't even have to open a shop; we could live off the profits."

Maximilian Carver threw his son an inquisitive glance.

"Listen. If you don't try it out, that bike will get covered in filth again and turn into a fossil."

"It already is," said Max, leaping onto the bicycle Jacob Fleischmann had never had the chance to use.

Max rode toward the town along the beach road, with its long row of houses similar to the Carvers' new home. The road led straight to the entrance of the small bay and the harbor used by fishermen. There were only four or five boats moored along the ancient docks, mostly small wooden rowing boats, no more than four meters long, which the local fishermen used, casting their old nets into the sea about a hundred meters from the coastline.

Max dodged through the maze of boats being repaired on the docks and the piles of wooden crates from the local fish market. With his eyes fixed on the beacon at the end, he set off along the breakwater that curved around the port like a half-moon. When he got there, he left the bike leaning against the side of the beacon and sat down to rest on one of the boulders on the seaward side of the breakwater, which had been eroded by the force of the waves. From there he could gaze at the dazzling light of the ocean spreading out before him toward eternity.

He'd been sitting there only a few moments when he saw another bicycle approaching along the quay. On the bike rode a tall, slim boy who, Max reckoned, must have been sixteen or seventeen. He rode up to the beacon and left his bike next to Max's. Then he pushed a shock of hair away from his face and walked over to where Max was sitting.

"Hello there. Have you just moved into the house at the end of the beach?"

Max nodded. "I'm Max."

The boy had deeply tanned skin and penetrating green eyes. He held out his hand.

"Roland. Welcome to Boring-on-Sea."

Max smiled and shook Roland's hand.

"How's the house? Do you like it?" asked the boy.

"Opinion is divided. My father loves it. The rest of the family doesn't see it that way," Max explained.

"I met your father a few months ago, when he came to the town," said Roland. "He seemed like good fun. A watchmaker, isn't that right?"

Max nodded again. "Yes, he is good fun...sometimes.

Other times he gets silly ideas into his head, like moving here."

"Why did you move?" asked Roland.

"The war," replied Max. "My father thinks it isn't a good time to be living in the city. I suppose he's right."

"The war," Roland repeated, his eyes downcast. "I'll be called up in September."

Max was at a loss for words. Noticing his silence, Roland smiled.

"It has its plus side," he added. "This could be the last summer I have to spend in this place."

Max smiled back timidly, thinking that in a few years' time, if the war hadn't ended, he would also have to enlist. Even on a radiant day such as this, the specter of war shrouded the future in darkness.

"I suppose you haven't seen the town yet," said Roland.

Max shook his head.

"Right. Get on your bike. I'm giving you the guided tour."

♦ ♦ ♦

Max had to struggle to keep up with Roland. They'd ridden only about two hundred meters from the end of the breakwater, and already he could feel sweat sliding down his forehead and his body. Roland turned and gave him a teasing grin.

"Lack of practice, eh? Life in the big city knock you out of shape?" he shouted without slowing down.

Max followed Roland along the promenade and into the streets of the town. When Max began to flag, Roland reduced his speed and stopped in the middle of a square by a large stone fountain from which fresh water gushed invitingly.

"I wouldn't recommend a drink," said Roland, reading his thoughts. "You'll get a stitch if you drink now."

Max took a deep breath and dipped his head under the jet of cold water.

"We'll go slower," Roland conceded.

Max kept his head immersed in the basin for a few seconds, then straightened up, water dripping down his head and onto his clothes.

"I didn't think you'd even last that long, to tell you the truth. This," he said pointing around him, "is the center of town. The main square containing the town hall. That building over there is the court, but it's not used anymore. There's a market here on Sundays. And on summer evenings, they show films on the wall of the town hall. Usually old movies with the reels all jumbled up."

Max gave a little nod as he tried to recover his breath.

"Sounds amazing, doesn't it?" laughed Roland. "There's also a library, but I'll stick my hand in the fire if it has more than sixty books."

"And what do people do around here?" Max managed to say. "Other than cycle."

"Good question, Max. I see you're beginning to get the idea. Shall we go?"

Max sighed and they returned to their bikes.

"But this time *I* set the pace," Max demanded. Roland shrugged his shoulders and pedaled off.

◆ ◆ ◆

For a couple of hours Roland guided Max up and down the small town and the surrounding area. They gazed at the cliffs to the south. That was the best place to go snorkeling, Roland told him, pointing offshore. An old cargo ship had sunk there in 1918 and was now covered in all kinds of strange seaweed, like some underwater jungle. Roland explained that one night, during a terrible storm, the ship had run aground on the dangerous rocks that lay a few meters beneath the surface. The waves were so furious and the night so dark—lit only by occasional flashes of lightning—that all the crew members drowned. All except one. The sole survivor of the tragedy was an engineer who, as a way of thanking providence for saving his life, had settled in the town and built a lighthouse high up on the steep cliffs that had presided over the scene that night. That man, who was now fairly old, was still the keeper of the lighthouse and was none other than Roland's adoptive grandfather. After the shipwreck, a couple from the town had taken him to the hospital and looked after him until he made a full recovery. Some years later, the same couple died in a car accident, and the lighthouse keeper, Victor Kray, decided to take in their son, Roland, who was barely a year old at the time.

"I'm sorry," offered Max.

"Never mind. It was a long time ago. I barely remember a thing," replied Roland.

Roland now lived with the former engineer in the lighthouse cottage, although he spent most of his time in a hut he had built himself on the beach, at the foot of the cliffs. For all intents and purposes, the lighthouse keeper *was* his real grandfather. Roland's voice seemed to betray a slight bitterness as he recounted these facts. Max listened in silence, not daring to ask any questions.

After the story of the shipwreck, the two boys walked through the streets near the old church, and Max met some of the locals — kind people who were quick to welcome him to the town.

Before long, Max decided he didn't need to get to know

the whole town in one morning. He was exhausted. If, as it seemed, he was going to spend a few years there, there'd be plenty of time to discover its mysteries—if there were any to discover.

"That's true," Roland said, nodding. "Listen. In the summer, I go diving at the sunken ship almost every morning. Would you like to come with me tomorrow?"

"If you swim the way you ride a bike, I'll drown," said Max.

"I have an extra pair of flippers and a mask."

The offer was tempting.

"All right. Do I need to bring anything?"

Roland shook his head.

"I'll bring everything. Well…come to think of it, bring something to eat. I'll pick you up from your house at nine o'clock."

"Nine thirty."

"Don't oversleep."

As Max rode back toward the beach house, the church bells announced that it was three o'clock, and the sun began to hide behind a blanket of dark clouds that spoke of rain.

◆ ◆ ◆

Max could hear the storm creeping in behind him, its shadow casting a gloomy shroud over the surface of the road. He turned around briefly and caught a glimpse of the darkness clawing at his back. In just a few minutes the sky changed into a vault of lead and the sea took on a metallic tint like mercury. The first flashes of lightning were accompanied by gusts of wind that propelled the storm in from the sea. Max pedaled hard, but the rain caught him when he was still half a kilometer from home. When he reached the white fence, he looked as if he'd just emerged from the sea and was drenched to the bone. He left the bicycle in the shed and went into the house through the back door. The kitchen was deserted, but an appetizing smell wafted toward him. On the table, Max found a tray with sandwiches and a jug of homemade lemonade. Next to it was a note in Andrea Carver's elegant handwriting.

Max, this is your lunch. Your father and I will be in town all afternoon running errands. Don't even THINK of using the upstairs bathroom. Irina is coming with us.

Max left the note on the table and decided to take the tray up to his room. The morning's marathon had left him exhausted. The house was silent and it seemed he was alone. Alicia wasn't in, or else she'd locked herself in her room. Max went straight upstairs, changed into dry clothes, and lay on his bed. Outside, the rain was hammering down and the thunder rattled the windowpanes. Max turned on the small lamp on his bedside table and picked up the book on Copernicus his father had given him. He'd started reading the same paragraph at least four times, but his mind was elsewhere and the mysteries of the universe suddenly seemed too far removed from his own life. All he could think of was how much he was looking forward to going diving around the sunken ship with his new friend Roland the next morning. He wolfed down the sandwiches and then closed his eyes, listening to the rain drumming on the roof. He loved the sound of the rain and the water rushing through the gutter along the edge of the roof.

Whenever it poured like this, Max felt as if time was pausing. It was like a cease-fire during which you could stop whatever you were doing and just stand by a window for hours, watching the performance, an endless curtain of tears falling from heaven. He put the book back on the bedside table and turned off the light. Slowly, lulled by the hypnotic sound of the rain, he surrendered to sleep.

5

THE VOICES OF HIS FAMILY on the lower floor and the
sound of Irina running up and down the stairs woke Max.
It was already dark, but he could see through the window that the storm had passed, leaving a canopy of stars
behind it. He glanced at his watch: He'd slept for almost
six hours. Just as he was sitting up, he heard someone rapping on his door.

"Dinnertime, sleeping beauty," Maximilian Carver
called out from the other side.

For a second, Max wondered why his father sounded
so cheerful. Then he remembered the screening he had
promised them that morning at breakfast.

"I'll be right down," he replied, his mouth still feeling pasty from the sandwiches.

"You'd better," said the watchmaker as he went down the stairs.

Although he didn't feel the least bit hungry, Max came down to the kitchen and sat at the table with the rest of the family. Alicia stared idly at her plate, as usual, not touching her food. Irina was devouring her portion with relish and babbling to her loathsome cat, which sat at her feet, its eyes glued to her every movement. As they ate, Mr. Carver told them that he'd found an excellent property in the town's center where he'd be able to set up his shop and restart his business.

"And what have you done today, Max?" asked Andrea Carver.

"I've been into town." The rest of the family looked at him, expecting more details. "I met a boy named Roland. Tomorrow we're going diving."

"There, you see? Max has already made a friend," stated Maximilian Carver triumphantly. "Didn't I tell you?"

"And what's this Roland like, Max?" asked Andrea Carver.

"I don't know. He's friendly. He lives with his grand-father, the lighthouse keeper. He's been showing me around the town."

"And where did you say you were going diving?" asked his father.

"On the southern beach, on the other side of the port. Roland told me you can see the remains of a ship that sank there years ago."

"Can I come too?" Irina interrupted.

"No," said Andrea Carver quickly. "Won't it be dangerous, Max?"

"Mum..."

"All right," Andrea Carver conceded, "but be careful."

Max nodded.

"When I was young, I was a good diver," Mr. Carver began.

"Not now, darling," his wife interrupted. "Weren't you going to show us some films?"

Maximilian Carver shrugged and stood up, eager to show off his skills as a projectionist.

"Give your father a hand, Max."

Before doing as he was asked, Max glanced over at Alicia. She had been silent throughout the meal, and it was crystal clear from the look on her face that she was miles away, yet for some reason nobody else seemed to have noticed, or they preferred not to. Alicia momentarily returned his gaze.

"Do you want to come with us tomorrow?" he suggested. "You'll like Roland."

Alicia didn't reply but she gave the hint of a smile and her dark, enigmatic eyes lit up for a second.

◆ ◆ ◆

"Ready. Lights out," said Maximilian Carver as he finished threading the film into the projector. The machine looked as if it belonged in the age of Copernicus himself, and Max had his doubts as to whether it would actually work.

"What are we going to see?" asked Andrea Carver, holding Irina in her arms.

"I haven't a clue," the watchmaker confessed. "There's a box in the shed with dozens of reels and none of them is labeled. I chose a few at random. It wouldn't surprise me if we don't see anything at all. The emulsion used on film is very fragile and it could easily have been damaged after all these years. You see, the nitrates used in—"

"Dear . . ." Andrea Carver said sweetly but firmly.

"Right." The watchmaker nodded.

"What does *emulsion* mean?" Irina asked. "Aren't we going to see anything, then?"

"There's only one way to find out," Maximilian Carver replied as he turned on the projector.

A few moments later they heard what sounded like an old motorcycle engine struggling to start as the machine rattled to life. Suddenly the beam from the lens cut through the room like a spear of light. Max concentrated on the rectangle projected onto the white wall. It was like looking inside a magic lantern, never knowing what visions might emerge from its depths. He held his breath, and in a few moments the wall came alive with pictures.

◆ ◆ ◆

It didn't take long for Max to realize that the film they were watching didn't come from the storeroom of some old cinema. It was not a print of some famous film or even a forgotten reel from a silent movie. The blurred pictures, eaten away by time, showed that whoever had filmed these images was obviously an amateur.

"What is this?" asked Irina.

"I don't know, darling," answered her father.

The film was a rather clumsy attempt at depicting a walk through what looked like a forest. The person operating the camera advanced slowly through the trees, the images jerking from one place to another with sudden shifts in light and focus, so that it was difficult to pick out where this strange walk was taking place.

"But, what *is* this?" cried Irina, visibly disappointed. She looked at her father, who was staring in bewilderment at what appeared to be a strange—and, judging from the first minute, boring—film.

"I don't know," mumbled Maximilian Carver, despondent. "I wasn't expecting this.... Maybe it's just one of the Fleischmanns' home movies."

"Is that the people who used to live in this house before us?"

Max had also started to lose interest in the film when something caught his eye in the confused rush of images.

"What if you try another reel, dear?" Andrea Carver suggested, trying to keep her husband's spirits up.

"Wait..." Max interrupted as he recognized a familiar silhouette.

The camera had now left the forest and was heading toward an area surrounded by tall stone walls with a gate of spearheaded bars. Max knew this place; he'd been there only that morning.

Fascinated, Max watched as the camera operator appeared to stumble slightly and then entered the walled garden filled with statues.

"It looks like a graveyard," whispered Andrea Carver. "Dear, turn this off."

"Just a second," said Max.

The camera panned across the scene. In the film the garden didn't look as neglected as it had when Max

52

discovered it. Not a hint of weeds, and the stone surface of the ground was clean and smooth; someone had been keeping the place immaculate.

The camera paused at each of the statues standing at the cardinal points of the large star that was clearly visible at the base of the figures. Max recognized the white stone faces, the circus costumes. There was something unnerving about the rigid poses adopted by these ghostly figures and the theatrical expressions on their masklike faces.

The film went from one statue to another, capturing each member of the circus troupe without any cuts. The family watched the haunting scene in silence, no other sound in the room except the rattle of the projector.

Finally, the camera turned toward the center of the inlaid star. Standing with its back to the light was the figure of the smiling clown, around which all the other statues were arranged. Max studied its features and felt the same shudder running through his body as when he'd stood in front of it. There was something about the clown that didn't quite match what he remembered from his visit to the walled garden, but the poor quality of the film didn't give him a clear enough view to work out what it was. The Carvers continued sitting in silence as the last few frames ran across the projector's beam. Maximilian Carver stopped the machine and turned on the light.

"Jacob Fleischmann," Max finally murmured. "These were filmed by Dr. Fleischmann's son."

"We don't know that, Max," said his father, his tone somber.

They looked at each other but Max said nothing. He started thinking about the boy who had drowned over ten years ago only meters away on that same beach. It seemed to him as if the boy's presence filled every corner of the house, making Max feel like an intruder. Maybe he was sleeping in what used to be his bed.

"Can we see some more?" Max asked hesitantly.

The watchmaker caught the darting looks his wife was giving him.

"I don't think that's a good idea, Max."

Without another word, Maximilian Carver began to dismantle the projector, and his wife picked up Irina and carried her upstairs to bed.

"Can I sleep with you?" asked Irina, hugging her mother.

"Leave this," said Max to his father. "I'll put it away."

Maximilian looked at his son, intrigued, but then patted him on the back.

"Don't do anything I wouldn't do," he whispered.

The watchmaker turned to his daughter. "Good night, Alicia."

"Good night, Dad," she replied, watching her father as he climbed the stairs. He looked tired and disappointed.

When the watchmaker's footsteps could no longer be heard, Alicia turned and fixed her eyes on Max.

"Is something wrong?" asked Max.

Alicia leaned toward him. Sometimes his sister had a peculiar intensity to her, as if she could shatter glass with a single glance.

"Promise me you won't tell anyone what I'm about to tell you," she said.

"But..."

"Promise. On your life."

Max sighed. "This better be good. Okay. I promise. What is it?"

Alicia shot one last look at the top of the stairs to make sure nobody could hear them.

"The clown. The one in the film..." she began.

Max didn't like where this was going.

"What about it?"

"I've seen it before."

"You've been to the garden of statues?"

Alicia shook her head, confused.

"What garden? No. I mean I've seen it before."

"Where?"

Alicia hesitated. "In a dream."

Max looked into Alicia's eyes. She was deadly serious about this. He felt a chill down his spine.

"When did you see him?" asked Max, his heart beating faster.

"The night before we came here."

It was difficult to read the emotions on Alicia's face, but Max thought he noticed a hint of fear in her eyes.

"Tell me about it," Max asked. "What exactly happened in your dream?"

"It's strange, but in the dream he was...I don't know...different," said Alicia.

"Different?" asked Max. "How?"

"Well, he wasn't a clown," she said, shrugging her shoulders, as if it didn't matter, but her voice was shaking. "Don't you believe me?"

"Yes, I believe you," Max said.

"Do you think it means anything?"

"No," Max said. "It was just a dream. I wouldn't worry about it."

Max smiled reassuringly at her. He had picked up this trick from his father, who was a master. You just had to pretend to be absolutely calm and positive about something, and then people would believe you. For the coup de grace, he placed his hand on Alicia's arm and gently squeezed it. His father used that one on his mother all the time.

"I guess you're right," Alicia agreed, suddenly embarrassed. "You won't tell anybody, will you?"

"Course not."

"I'd better go to bed, too. Long day..."

"Sounds like a good idea."

Alicia walked toward the stairs.

"By the way, is the plan for tomorrow still on? Diving...?" she asked.

Max was surprised she was holding him to his offer. He nodded.

"Of course. Shall I wake you up?"

Alicia smiled shyly at her younger brother. It was the first time Max had seen her give a proper smile in months. It felt good.

"I'll be awake," she replied. "Good night, Max. And thanks."

"Good night, Alicia."

Max waited until he heard the door to Alicia's room close, then he sat in the armchair next to the projector. From there he could hear the murmur of his parents speaking in low voices. The rest of the house sank slowly into the silence of night, disturbed only by the sound of the waves breaking on the beach. Suddenly Max felt a presence right behind him. He turned around. Someone was looking at him from the foot of the stairs.

The shining, yellow eyes of Irina's cat observed him from the gloom.

"Get out," Max spat.

The cat kept its eyes on Max for a few seconds longer. They were lifeless and cold, like doll's eyes. Max stood and faced the beast.

"I said out."

The cat appeared to smile, if such a thing were possible, then slowly withdrew into the shadows. What a time for Irina to bring that *thing* into their home.... Max started putting away the projector and the films. The thought of returning them all to the garden shed and having to go outdoors in the pitch dark wasn't tempting, so he decided he would do that in the morning. He turned off the lights and went up to his bedroom. As he opened the door, he imagined Jacob Fleischmann placing his hand on that same handle years ago, entering what was now to be his room. He lay down on the bed and turned off his bedside lamp. For a while he listened to the thousand tiny noises a house makes when it thinks nobody is listening. He closed his eyes and tried to imagine he was back in the city walking along the streets, passing familiar faces and places he used to go to. He smiled to himself and slowly, without realizing, he began to slip into sleep.

The last image that flitted through his mind before he succumbed was his sister Alicia's unexpected smile. It had been an apparently insignificant gesture, but for some reason, Max felt as if a door had opened between them and that, from that night on, he would never again view his sister as a stranger.

6

ALICIA AWOKE SHORTLY after sunrise to find two amber eyes staring intently at her from the window. She sat up with a jerk. The cat calmly padded away from the window-sill. Since they had arrived in their new home, Alicia had learned to detest the animal, with its superior attitude and that penetrating smell that seemed to announce its presence before it even walked into a room. This wasn't the first time she'd caught it watching her. From the moment Irina had managed to introduce the feline into the house, Alicia had noticed that it would often spend whole minutes not moving at all, vigilant, spying on the movements of some family member from a doorway or lying hidden in the shadows. She usually loved animals, but for once, she wasn't quite sure why, Alicia secretly relished the thought that some stray dog might finish off the beast during one of its nightly outings.

Outside, the sky was losing the purple hue of dawn, and the first rays of a blazing sun pierced the forest that extended beyond the walled garden. There were still at least two hours before Max's new friend was due to pick them up. Alicia slipped under the sheets again and considered going back to sleep. Morning naps were her favorite and they always brought the best dreams. She closed her eyes and listened to the muffled sound of the waves on the beach, yet sleep seemed to elude her. She started wondering about Max's friend Roland. She climbed out of bed, walked to her wardrobe, and studied her collection of clothes. They still smelled of the city. Suddenly two hours didn't seem like enough time to decide what she was going to wear.

But only an hour later, Max rapped gently on her door. "Morning...Roland's here," he called.

"I'll be straight down."

Alicia gave herself one last look in the mirror and sighed, then she tiptoed down the stairs. Max and his friend were waiting for her on the porch. Before going out she stopped in the hallway and listened to the two boys chatting. She took a deep breath and opened the door.

Max was leaning on the railings. He turned around and smiled at her. Next to him stood a boy with tanned skin and straw-colored hair who was almost half a head taller than Max. He smiled shyly at her. He had the greenest eyes she had ever seen.

"This is Roland," said Max. "Roland, my sister Alicia."

Roland nodded politely and turned toward the bicycles, but the look that had passed between the two did not go unnoticed by Max. He smiled to himself. This outing was going to be more fun than he'd thought.

"How are we going to do this?" asked Alicia. "There are only two bikes."

"I think Roland could take you on his," replied Max. "What do you think, Roland?"

Roland stared at the ground. "Yes, of course," he mumbled. "But you'll have to carry the gear."

Max clamped Roland's diving equipment onto the small rack behind his seat. He knew there was another bicycle in the shed, but the thought of Roland having to transport his sister amused him. Alicia sat on the crossbar and held on to Roland's shoulders. Despite Roland's tan, Max noticed how he was struggling not to blush.

"Ready," said Alicia. "I hope I'm not too heavy."

"Let's go," said Max, and he began pedaling along the road.

After a while, Roland overtook him and, once more, Max had to push himself in order not to be left behind.

"Are you all right there?" Roland asked Alicia.

Alicia nodded and watched as the house by the beach disappeared into the distance.

♦ ♦ ♦

The southern beach, on the other side of the town, was shaped like a vast crescent moon. Beyond the strip of white sand, the shoreline was covered with shiny pebbles smoothed by the sea. Behind the beach, rising almost vertically, loomed a wall of craggy cliffs, on top of which stood the lighthouse, dark and solitary.

"That's my grandfather's lighthouse," said Roland, pointing to it as they left their bicycles by one of the paths leading down through the rocks to the beach.

"Do you both live there?" asked Alicia.

"More or less," Roland answered. "Over time I've built myself a hut down on the beach. I'd almost say it's my home now."

"Your own beach hut?" Alicia asked, trying to spot it.

"You won't see it from here," Roland explained. "It was an old fisherman's hut that had been abandoned. I fixed it up and now it's not too bad. You'll be able to see it in a minute."

Roland led them onto the beach, where he removed his sandals. The sun was already quite high and the sea shone like liquid silver. The beach was deserted and a salty breeze blew in from the water. Roland pointed toward the shoreline and the larger stones glowing beneath the surf.

"Mind these stones. I'm used to them, but it's easy to trip if you're not."

Alicia and her brother followed Roland along the beach to his hut. It was a small wooden cabin painted blue and red with a narrow porch. Max noticed a rusty lamp hanging from a chain.

"That's from the ship," Roland explained. "I've brought up a whole pile of stuff from down there. What do you think of it?"

"It's fantastic," exclaimed Alicia. "Do you sleep here?"

"Mostly in the summer. In winter it gets too cold and anyway, I don't like leaving my grandfather alone up there."

Roland opened the door and let Alicia and Max go in first.

"Welcome to my palace."

The inside of the hut was like some old bazaar filled with nautical antiques. The booty Roland had pulled out of the ocean over the years shone in the dark like a mysterious hoard of treasure.

"It's mostly cheap nonsense," said Roland, "but I like to collect it. Maybe we'll find something today."

The hut also contained an old cupboard, a table, a few chairs, and a rickety bed. Above the bed were shelves with a few books and an oil lamp.

"I'd love to have a house like this," said Max.

Roland smiled skeptically.

"I'm open to offers," he joked, clearly proud of the impression the hut had made on his friends. "Right, let's go."

They followed Roland to the water's edge, and he began to untie the bundle containing his diving gear.

"The ship lies about twenty-five or thirty meters off the shore. The water gets deep very quickly; three meters in and you can't touch the bottom. The hull is about ten meters down," Roland explained.

Max and Alicia exchanged a look.

"Yes," said Roland, noticing. "It's not a good idea to try to reach the bottom the first time you dive. Sometimes, when there's a heavy swell, the currents can be dangerous. Once I nearly scared myself to death."

Roland handed Max a mask and a pair of flippers.

"There's only enough equipment for two. Who's coming down first?"

Alicia pointed to Max.

"Thank you," muttered Max.

"Don't worry," Roland reassured him. "You just have to get started. The first time I went down I nearly had a fit. There was a gigantic moray eel in one of the chimneys."

"A what?" Max jumped.

"Nothing," Roland replied. "I'm only joking. There aren't any strange creatures down there, I promise. Which is odd, because usually sunken ships are like a kind of aquarium. But not this one. I suppose they don't like it there. You're not going to get scared now, are you?"

"Scared?" said Max. "Me?"

Although Max was busy putting on his flippers, he noticed that Roland was having a good look at his sister as she removed her cotton dress, revealing her white bathing costume—the only one she had—and waded into the sea.

"Hey," Max hissed at him. "She's my sister, not a piece of cake. Okay?"

Roland threw him a cheeky grin.

"You're the one who invited her, not me," he replied with a catlike smile.

"Let's get in the water," said Max quickly. "It will do you good."

Alicia turned and when she saw them in their masks and snorkels, she started to grin.

"You should see yourselves!" she said, unable to stop herself from laughing.

Max and Roland looked at one another through their masks.

"Before we go," said Max. "I've never done this before. Swim underwater, I mean. I've swum in swimming pools, but I'm not sure that I'll know..."

Roland rolled his eyes.

"Do you know how to hold your breath underwater?" he asked.

"I said I didn't know how to dive, not that I was an idiot," replied Max.

"Well, if you know how to hold your breath, you know how to swim underwater," Roland said.

"Be careful," Alicia said. "Listen, Max, are you sure this is a good idea?"

"We'll be fine," Roland assured her, turning to Max and patting him on the shoulder. "You first, my captain."

◆ ◆ ◆

For the first time in his life, Max submerged himself beneath the surface of the sea and a whole universe of light and shadow—more amazing than anything he had imagined—opened up before his eyes. Sunbeams filtered through the water in veils of nebulous light that swayed gently with the motion of the waves, and the surface was transformed into an opaque, dancing mirror. Max held his breath for a few more seconds, then reemerged for air. A few meters behind, Roland was watching him attentively.

"Everything all right?" he asked.

Max nodded enthusiastically.

"You see? It's easy. Swim next to me," Roland advised him before diving again.

Max took a last look at the shore and saw Alicia waving at him. He waved back, then swam off next to his friend, heading for the open sea. Roland guided him to a point that seemed quite far from the beach, although Max knew it was barely thirty meters away. At sea level, distances seemed to grow. Roland touched his arm and pointed toward the ocean bed. Max breathed in and put his head underwater, adjusting his diving mask. His eyes took a few seconds to get used to the watery gloom. Only then was he able to admire the spectacle of the sunken shell of the ship, lying on its side and enveloped in a spectral light. The ship must have been about fifty meters long, perhaps more, and had a large crack all the way from the bow to the bilge, a gaping black wound inflicted by the sharp claws of the rocks hidden in the shallows. On the bow, under a layer of copper-colored rust and swaying seaweed, Max could make out the ship's name, the *Orpheus*.

The *Orpheus* looked as if she'd been an old freighter,

not a passenger ship. Her splintered steel was covered in algae but, just as Roland had said, there wasn't a single fish swimming around the hull. The two friends swam over her, keeping to the surface and stopping every now and then to have a good look at the remains of the wreck. Roland had said the ship lay about ten meters down, but from the surface, the distance seemed vast. Max wondered how Roland had managed to recover all the objects they'd seen in his hut. As if he'd read Max's thoughts, his friend signaled to him to wait on the surface and then dived down, kicking powerfully with his flippers.

Max watched Roland descend until he could touch the hull of the *Orpheus* with his fingertips. Then Roland slowly crept toward the platform that had once been the ship's bridge, holding on to anything he could grasp. From his position Max could make out the wheel at the helm and other instruments that were still inside the vessel. Roland swam toward the doorway of the bridge and went in. Max felt a pang of anxiety as he saw his friend disappear into the sunken ship. While Roland moved about inside the bridge, Max kept his eyes riveted to the entrance, wondering what he would do if anything happened. A few seconds later, Roland emerged and swam quickly up to him, a garland of bubbles rising behind him. Max lifted his head out of the water and breathed deeply. Roland's face appeared just a meter away, grinning from ear to ear.

"Surprise!" he yelled.

Max saw he was holding something in his hand.

"What's that?" he asked, pointing to the strange metal object Roland had salvaged from the bridge.

"A sextant."

Max raised his eyebrows. He had no idea what it was.

"A sextant is a gadget that's used to calculate your position in the sea," Roland explained, his voice faltering after the effort of holding his breath for almost a minute. "I'm going down again. Hold it for me."

Max was about to protest but Roland plunged down before he could even open his mouth. He inhaled deeply and dipped his head below the surface to follow Roland's dive. This time, his friend swam the whole length of the hull until he reached the stern. Max watched Roland swim up to a porthole and try to look inside the ship. Max held his breath until his lungs were burning, then let out all the air, ready to resurface and breathe again. But in that last second his eyes caught sight of something that chilled his blood.

Through the darkness, he could see an old flag undulating in the water—rotten and ragged, it was fastened to a mast on the stern of the *Orpheus*. Max observed it carefully and recognized the faded symbol that was still visible: a six-pointed star within a circle. He felt a shiver course through his body. He had seen that symbol before, above the spear-shaped tips of the gate in the garden of statues.

Roland's sextant slipped from his fingers and sank down to the shadows below. Overcome by an inexplicable fear, Max swam back to the shore as fast as he could.

◆ ◆ ◆

Half an hour later, sitting in the shade of the porch at the beach hut, Roland and Max watched Alicia as she collected seashells from among the pebbles on the shore.

"Are you sure you've seen that symbol before, Max?"

Max nodded.

"Sometimes, underwater, things are not what they seem—" Roland began.

"I know what I saw," Max interrupted. "Okay?"

"Okay," Roland conceded. "You saw a symbol that, according to you, is also in that graveyard behind your house. So what?"

Max stood up and faced his friend.

"So what? Do you want me to repeat the whole story?"

Max had spent the last twenty-five minutes telling

Roland everything he knew about the walled garden, including Jacob Fleischmann's film.

"There's no need," Roland replied drily.

"Then how can you possibly not believe me?" snapped Max. "Do you think I'm inventing all this?"

"I'm not saying I don't believe you, Max," said Roland, smiling softly at Alicia, who had returned from her walk with a little bag of shells. "Any luck?"

"This beach is a real treasure trove," Alicia replied, jangling the bag containing her stash.

Max rolled his eyes impatiently.

"You believe me, then?" he retorted, staring at Roland insistently.

His friend returned his gaze but said nothing for a while.

"I believe you, Max," he said eventually, turning to look at the horizon, unable to hide a shadow of sadness in his expression. Alicia noticed the change in Roland's face.

"Max told me your grandfather was traveling on the ship the night it sank," she said, placing her hand on his shoulder.

Roland nodded vaguely.

"He was the only survivor."

"What happened?" asked Alicia. "I'm sorry. Perhaps you don't want to talk about it."

Roland shook his head.

"No, I don't mind," he said. Max was looking at him expectantly. "And it's not that I don't believe your story, Max. It's just that it's not the first time someone has talked to me about that symbol."

"Who else has seen it?" asked Max, openmouthed. "Who's talked to you about it?"

"My grandfather. Ever since I was a child." Roland pointed toward the inside of the hut. "It's getting chilly. Let's go in and I'll tell you the story about this ship."

◆ ◆ ◆

At first, Irina thought it was her mother's voice she'd heard downstairs. Andrea Carver often talked to herself while she was busy around the house, and no one was surprised by her habit of voicing her thoughts aloud. An instant later, however, Irina saw her mother through the window, standing in the front yard, saying good-bye to her father. The watchmaker was setting off toward the town with one of the porters who had helped them bring the luggage from the station a few days earlier. Irina realized then that she was alone inside the house and therefore the voice she thought she'd heard must have been imaginary. Until she heard it again, this time in her bedroom, like a whisper filtering through the walls.

72

The voice seemed to come from far away, the words impossible to decipher. She stood in the center of the room, motionless. She heard the voice again. Whispering. It was coming from inside the wardrobe. For the first time since she'd arrived at the beach house, Irina was afraid. She stared at the door of the wardrobe and noticed there was a key in the lock. Without thinking twice, she ran over and hurriedly turned the key to make sure it was properly locked. She stepped back and took a deep breath. But then she heard the sound again and realized it wasn't just one voice but several, all whispering at the same time.

"Irina?" her mother called from downstairs. "Irina, could you come down and help me for a minute?"

Never had Irina been so willing to help her mother, no matter what the task was that awaited her. She was about to leave the room when suddenly she felt an icy breeze on her face. It swept through the bedroom, slamming the door shut. Irina ran toward the door and struggled with the knob, which seemed to be stuck. As she was trying in vain to open it, she heard the key in the wardrobe door slowly turning behind her. Irina stood against the door of her room, too afraid to look. She closed her eyes tight, and her hands were shaking. The voices, which appeared to emanate from the very depths of the house, seemed much closer now. And this time, they were laughing.

♦ ♦ ♦

"When I was a child," Roland explained, "my grandfather told me the story so many times that over the years I've often dreamed about it. It all began when I came to live in this town, many years ago, after my parents died in a car accident."

"I'm sorry, Roland," Alicia interrupted, guessing that, despite his friendly smile and his willingness to tell them the story about his grandfather and the ship, revisiting these memories was probably harder for him than he cared to show.

"I was very young. I barely remember them," said Roland, avoiding Alicia's eyes, for he knew she was not going to believe his white lie.

"So what happened then?" Max insisted.

Alicia looked daggers at her brother.

"Granddad took care of me and I moved into the lighthouse cottage with him. He was an engineer and he'd been the lighthouse keeper on this stretch of coast for years. The local council had given him the job for life because he'd practically built the lighthouse with his bare hands, back in 1919. It's a bizarre story, you'll see.

"On June 23, 1918, my grandfather boarded the *Orpheus*, but he traveled undercover. The *Orpheus* wasn't a passenger ship, but a cargo ship with a bad reputation. Her captain was a drunken Dutchman who was corrupt

74

through and through and used to rent the ship out to the highest bidder. The Dutchman's favorite clients were usually smugglers who wanted to cross the Channel without a lot of questions being asked or any official paperwork being involved. Still, with time business had begun to fall off and the Flying Dutchman, as my grandfather called him, had to find other shady deals to pay off the gambling debts he had accumulated. It seems that on one of the nights when his luck was down—which was most nights—the captain lost his shirt in a card game to someone named Mr. Cain. This Mr. Cain was the owner of a traveling circus. As payment for his debt he demanded that the Dutchman take his entire company on board his ship and transport them secretly across the Channel. Mr. Cain's so-called circus had more to hide than a few simple sideshows, and they needed to disappear as soon as possible. Illegally, of course. The Dutchman agreed. What else could he do? Either he accepted or he lost his ship.

"Just a moment," Max interrupted. "What did your grandfather have to do with all this?"

"I'm getting there," Roland continued. "As I said, this Mr. Cain—although that wasn't his real name—had a lot to hide. My grandfather had been following his trail for some time. They had some unfinished business, and my grandfather thought that if Mr. Cain and his minions crossed the Channel, his chance of catching them would evaporate forever."

"Is that why he went on board the *Orpheus*?" asked Max. "As a stowaway?"

Roland nodded.

"There's something else I don't understand," said Alicia. "Why didn't he just call the authorities? He was an engineer, not a detective. What sort of unfinished business did he have with this Mr. Cain?"

"May I finish the story?" asked Roland.

Max and his sister nodded.

"Right. The fact is that he did board the ship. The *Orpheus* set sail at noon and the captain hoped to reach his destination in the dead of night, but things got complicated. A storm broke out just after midnight, sending the ship toward the coast. The *Orpheus* crashed against the rocks submerged near the cliff and sank in a matter of minutes. My grandfather's life was saved because he was hiding in a lifeboat. Everybody else on board drowned."

Max gulped.

"Do you mean to say the bodies are still down there?"

"No," Roland replied. "The following day, at dawn, a fog swept over the coast. The local fishermen found my granddad, unconscious, on this beach. When the fog lifted, a few of them went out in their boats and searched the area around the shipwreck. They never found any bodies."

"But, then…" Max said in a low voice.

Roland gestured to Max to let him continue.

"My grandfather was taken to the town hospital and was delirious for days. When he recovered, he decided, as a token of his gratitude for the care he'd received, to build a lighthouse on the cliff top and prevent a similar tragedy from happening again. In time, he became the lighthouse keeper."

The three friends fell into a long silence after Roland ended his story. At last, Roland looked at Alicia, then at Max.

"Roland," said Max, trying to find words that would not upset his friend, "there's something in this story that doesn't quite add up. I don't think your grandfather has told you everything."

Roland remained silent. Then, smiling faintly, he nodded a few times, very slowly.

"I know," he murmured. "I know."

◆ ◆ ◆

Irina felt her hands go numb as she tried, unsuccessfully, to force open the door. She turned around, gasping, and leaned against it, pushing with all her might. She couldn't help staring at the key that was slowly turning in the wardrobe lock.

At last the key stopped moving and, as if pushed out by invisible fingers, it fell to the floor. Little by little, the door began to creak open. Irina tried to scream but she couldn't find enough breath even to whisper.

From the darkness of the wardrobe, a shape emerged. For a second she felt as if her heart was going to stop from sheer panic. Then she sighed. It was her cat. It was only her cat. She took a deep breath and knelt down to pick it up but then she noticed that behind the cat, at the back of the wardrobe, there was something, or someone, else. The cat opened its jaws, issued a deep, horrifying sound like the hiss of a snake, then melted into the darkness with its master. A smile filled with light appeared, and two glowing eyes like liquid gold settled on hers as the voices pronounced her name in unison. Irina screamed and threw herself against the bedroom door; this time it gave way, and she fell onto the floor of the hallway. Without losing a second, she hurled herself down the stairs, feeling the cold air of the voices on the nape of her neck.

◆ ◆ ◆

Andrea Carver was walking through the front doorway when she heard the scream. She looked up and watched in horror as Irina jumped from the top of the stairs, her face frozen in fear. She called out, but it was too late. The child came tumbling down, step after step, like a dead weight. Andrea Carver rushed toward her daughter and cradled her head. A tear of blood ran across Irina's forehead. Mrs. Carver touched her neck and felt her pulse: It was weak. Fighting hysteria, she lifted her daughter's body and tried to think what she should do next.

As the worst five seconds of her life passed before her, Andrea Carver raised her eyes and looked up at the top of the stairs. Sitting on the last step was Irina's cat and it was staring at her. Andrea held the animal's cruel, mocking gaze for a brief moment, and then, feeling her daughter's body shudder in her arms, she reacted and hurried to the telephone.

7

As they approached the beach house, Max noticed a strange car parked out in front. Roland noticed it too, and frowned.

"That's Dr. Roberts' car," Roland said.

Alicia went pale.

"Something's wrong," she whispered.

Roland raced ahead and Max had trouble catching up with him, even though his friend was also carrying Alicia. When they were just a few meters from the house, Alicia jumped off the bicycle and ran toward the porch. Max, panting, followed her while Roland took care of the bicycles. Maximilian Carver, ashen-faced and with a glazed look in his eyes, greeted them at the door.

"What's happened?" Alicia said, her voice trembling.

Her father hugged her. Alicia let him wrap his arms around her—his hands were shaking and when he spoke his voice kept breaking. Max felt something tighten in his throat. He had never seen his father like this.

"Irina's had an accident. She's in a coma. We're waiting for the ambulance to take her to the hospital."

"Is Mum all right?" asked Alicia.

"She's inside with Irina and the doctor. There's nothing else we can do here," replied the watchmaker, lowering his eyes.

Roland stood quietly at the foot of the porch.

"Will she be all right?" asked Max, immediately realizing that the question was stupid, given the circumstances.

"We don't know," Maximilian Carver muttered. He tried to smile at them before going back into the house. "I'll see if your mother needs anything."

The three friends stood there, glued to the spot. At first no one said a word but then Roland spoke up.

"I'm sorry..."

Alicia nodded in response. Shortly afterward, the ambulance arrived and stopped outside the house and the doctor came out to meet it. It took only a few minutes for the two paramedics to go inside, then emerge, carrying Irina on a stretcher, wrapped in a blanket. Max caught a glimpse of his little sister's face, which was as white as a sheet, and felt his stomach churn. Andrea Carver, her face tense and her eyes red and swollen, got into the ambulance and peered out despairingly at Alicia and Max. The ambulance crew rushed to their seats. Maximilian Carver walked over to his two children.

"I don't like leaving you on your own. There's a small hotel in the town. Perhaps..."

"We'll be fine, Dad. Don't worry about that now," Alicia replied.

"I'll call from the hospital and give you the number. I don't know how long we'll be there, I don't know whether there's anything..."

"Just go, Dad." Alicia hugged her father. "Everything will be all right."

Trying to hold back his tears, Maximilian Carver climbed into the ambulance. The three friends stood quietly, watching the vehicle's lights disappearing into the distance as the last rays of sun lingered in the violet dusk.

"Everything will be all right," Alicia repeated to herself.

◆ ◆ ◆

Once they'd found some dry clothes (Alicia lent Roland a pair of old trousers and a shirt belonging to her father), the wait for news seemed endless. The smiling moons on Max's watch showed it was a few minutes to eleven o'clock when the phone finally rang. Alicia, who was sitting between Roland and Max on the porch steps, jumped up and ran into the house. Before the phone rang a second time, she picked up the receiver.

"All right," she said, nodding at Max and Roland. "How's Mum?"

Max could hear the rumble of his father's voice down the line.

"Don't worry," said Alicia. "No. There's no need. Yes, we'll be fine. Call again tomorrow." Alicia paused. "I will," she assured him. "Me too. Good night, Dad."

She hung up and looked at her brother.

"Irina is being kept under observation," she explained. "The doctors say she has a concussion. She's still in a coma but they say she'll recover."

"Are you sure that's what they said?" Max replied. "What about Mum?"

"You can imagine. They're going to spend the night there because Mum doesn't want to go to a hotel. They'll call us again tomorrow at ten."

"What will we do now?" Roland asked worriedly.

Alicia shrugged her shoulders.

"Is anyone hungry?" she asked the two boys.

Max felt surprisingly hungry. Alicia stifled a yawn; she looked exhausted.

"I think it would do us all good to have some dinner," she concluded. "Anyone disagree?"

It took Max a few minutes to prepare some sandwiches while Alicia made lemonade. They had dinner on the porch, sitting on the bench, under the faint glow of the lamp that swayed in the night breeze, wrapped in a dancing cloud of moths. The full moon rose high above the sea, transforming the water's surface into a lake of luminous metal that stretched toward infinity. They ate in silence, gazing at the ocean and listening to the soft swell of the waves.

"I don't think I'll sleep a wink tonight," said Alicia, sitting up and scanning the horizon.

"I don't think any of us will," Max agreed.

"I have an idea," said Roland, a conspiratorial smile on his lips. "Have you ever swum at night?"

"Are you joking?" Max retorted.

Without saying a word, Alicia gave the two boys a look, her eyes shining and mysterious, then got up and walked calmly toward the beach. Max watched in astonishment as his sister crossed the sand and, without turning round, slipped off her white cotton dress. She stood at the water's edge for a moment, her pale skin gleaming under the bluish light of the moon and then, slowly, she submerged her body into the immense pool of light.

"Aren't you coming, Max?" said Roland, following Alicia's footsteps on the sand.

Max didn't reply, but he shook his head and watched as his friend dived in. He could hear his sister's laughter amid the whispering sounds of the sea.

He sat quietly on the porch, trying to decide whether or not he was saddened by the strong spark between Roland and his sister, a chemistry that escaped all definition and from which he knew he was excluded. While he watched them playing around in the water, Max knew, probably even before they were aware of it, that a lasting bond was growing between them, a bond that would unite them that summer and that seemed as inevitable as destiny.

As he thought about these things, Max's mind turned to the shadows of a war that was being fought so close and yet so far from that beach, a faceless war that would soon lay claim to his friend Roland and, perhaps, even to him. He also thought about all the events that had happened during that long day, from his sighting of the ghostly *Orpheus* beneath the sea to Roland's story in the beach hut and Irina's accident. Away from the laughter of Alicia and Roland, a deep anxiety took hold of him. For the first time in his life, he felt that time was going faster than he wished it to and he could no longer take refuge in his dreams. The wheel of fortune had started to turn, and this time he could not stop it.

◆ ◆ ◆

Later, by the light of a bonfire they had built on the beach, Alicia, Roland, and Max spoke about what had been going through their minds over the last few hours. The golden glow of the fire was reflected on the damp, shining faces of Alicia and Roland. Max sat observing them for a long while before deciding to speak.

"I don't know how to explain this, but I think something's going on," he began. "I don't know what it is, but there are too many coincidences. The statues, that symbol, the ship..."

Max thought they'd both contradict him, or else reassure him with the sensible words that escaped him, making him see that his anxiety was only the result of a long day in which too many things had happened. But they didn't. Instead, both Alicia and Roland nodded, their eyes still fixed on the fire.

"You told me you dreamed about that clown, didn't you?" Max asked.

Again Alicia nodded.

"There's something I didn't tell you before," Max went on. "Last night, when you all went to bed, I had another look at the film Jacob Fleischmann took in the walled garden. I was in that garden yesterday morning. The statues were in different positions. I don't know...it's as if they've moved. What I saw is not what was in the film."

Alicia turned her eyes toward Roland, who seemed mesmerized by the dancing flames.

"Roland, has your grandfather ever talked to you about all this?"

The boy didn't seem to have heard her question. Alicia put her hand on his and he looked up.

"I've dreamed about that clown every summer since I was five," he said in a muted tone.

Max saw the fear in his face.

"I think we should talk to your grandfather."

Roland gave a slight nod.

"Tomorrow," he promised, his voice barely audible. "Tomorrow."

8

Shortly before daybreak, Roland got on his bike and rode back toward the lighthouse cottage. As he traveled along the beach road, a pale amber glow began to tint the covering of low clouds. His mind raced with worry and his nerves were on edge. He pedaled as fast as he could in the vain hope that the physical exertion might dispel the hundreds of questions and fears colliding inside him.

Once he'd crossed the harbor and gone up the path to the lighthouse, Roland stopped to recover his breath. From the top of the cliff, the lighthouse beam sliced through the last shadows of the night like a blade of fire. He knew his grandfather would still be there, expectant, silent, and that he wouldn't leave his post until the darkness had vanished completely. For years, Roland had lived with the old man's unhealthy obsession without querying the reason or the logic of his behavior. It was simply something he'd accepted as a child, one more aspect of daily life he'd learned not to question.

As time went by, however, Roland had become aware that the old man's story didn't quite hold together. But never, until that day, had he wanted to admit to himself that his grandfather had lied to him or, at least, that he hadn't told him the whole truth. He didn't doubt his grandfather's integrity for one minute. In fact, over the years, his grandfather had gradually been disclosing the pieces of the jigsaw puzzle, at the center of which, he now realized, was the garden of statues. At times he did so through words spoken in dreams, more often through the half-formed replies to Roland's questions, but somehow Roland felt that if his grandfather was keeping him from his secret, he had done so only to protect him. This state of grace, however, appeared to be coming to an end, and it was time to face the truth.

Roland set off again, trying to put these thoughts behind him. He'd been awake for too long and his body was beginning to feel the strain. When he reached the lighthouse cottage, he left his bicycle leaning against the fence and went indoors without bothering to turn on the light. He climbed the stairs to his bedroom and collapsed on his bed like a deadweight.

From his bedroom window he could see the lighthouse itself, some thirty meters beyond the cottage, and behind the large windows of its tower, the motionless silhouette of his grandfather. Roland closed his eyes and tried to sleep.

The events of that day paraded through his mind, from the dive down to the *Orpheus* to the accident of Alicia and Max's younger sister. Roland thought it was both strange and somehow comforting to realize that just a few hours together had brought them so close. As he lay there in the solitude of his room, thinking about the brother and sister, he felt they had become his closest friends, two soul mates with whom, from that day on, he'd be able to share his secrets and fears.

He noticed that the very fact of thinking about them was enough to make him feel safe, as if he was not alone. In return, he felt deep loyalty and gratitude for the invisible pact that seemed to have bound them together that night on the beach.

When at last exhaustion won, Roland's last thoughts as he fell into a deep, refreshing sleep were not about the mysterious uncertainty that hung over them or the grim possibility that he would be called up to join the army that coming autumn. That night, Roland fell asleep in the arms of a vision that would stay with him for the rest of his life: Alicia, draped in moonlight, dipping her white skin into a sea of silver.

◆ ◆ ◆

Day broke under a blanket of dark, menacing clouds that stretched beyond the horizon. Leaning on the metal railing of the lighthouse tower, Victor Kray gazed down at the bay, thinking about how he'd learned to recognize the mysterious beauty of those leaden, storm-clad days that foretold the advent of summer on the coast.

From his vantage point, the town looked like a scale model meticulously assembled by a collector. Farther on, toward the north, the beach extended in an endless white line. On bright, sunny days, standing in the same place, Victor Kray was able to distinguish the shape of the *Orpheus* under the water, like a monstrous fossil wedged in the sand.

That morning, however, the sea was like a deep, murky lake. As he scanned its surface, Victor Kray thought about the last twenty-five years he'd spent in the lighthouse that he himself had built. Looking back, he felt as if every one of those years was like a heavy stone, weighing him down.

As time passed, the anguish of his never-ending wait

had led him to believe that perhaps it had all been a fantasy, that his obstinate obsession had turned him into a sentry who was guarding against a threat that was only imagined. But then the dreams had returned. The phantoms of the past had awoken from a sleep of many years and were once again haunting the corridors of his mind. And with them came the fear that he was now too old and too weak to confront his ancient enemy.

For years now he had barely slept more than two or three hours a day. Most of the time he was alone in the lighthouse. His grandson, Roland, spent a few nights a week in his beach hut, so it wasn't unusual that, for days at a time, they might have only a few minutes together. This distance from his own grandson, to which Victor Kray had voluntarily condemned himself, did at least give him some comfort, for he was sure that the pain he felt at not being able to share those years of the boy's life was the price he had to pay for Roland's safety and future happiness.

Despite all this, every time he looked down from his tower and saw the boy dive into the waters near the hull of the *Orpheus*, his blood froze. He had never wanted Roland to know how he felt, and ever since Roland was a child he'd always replied to his questions about the ship and the past, trying not to lie to him but, at the same time, never explaining the true nature of events. The day before, as he watched Roland and his two new friends on the beach, he had wondered whether that hadn't been a huge mistake.

Such thoughts kept him in the lighthouse longer than usual that morning. Normally, he returned home before eight, but when Victor Kray looked at his watch, it was already half past ten. He went down the metal stairs that spiraled around the tower and walked over to the cottage to make the most of the few hours' sleep he allowed himself. On the way, he saw Roland's bicycle and knew he'd come home last night.

As he stepped quietly into the house, trying not to disturb his grandson, he discovered that Roland was waiting for him, sitting in one of the old armchairs in the dining room.

"I couldn't sleep, Granddad," said Roland. "I was out like a light for a couple of hours, but then suddenly I woke up and couldn't get back to sleep."

"I know what that feels like," Victor Kray replied. "But I have a trick that never fails."

"What's that?" asked Roland.

The old man gave him one of his mischievous smiles, which took sixty years off him.

"I start cooking. Are you hungry?"

Roland considered his question. Yes, the thought of buttered toast with jam and fried eggs tickled his stomach, so immediately he agreed.

"Right," said Victor Kray. "You'll be first mate. Let's get cracking."

Roland followed his grandfather into the kitchen, ready for his instructions.

"I'm the engineer," Victor Kray said, "so I'll fry the eggs. You make the toast."

In just a few minutes, grandfather and grandson managed to fill the kitchen with smoke and the irresistible aroma of a freshly made breakfast. They sat opposite one another at the kitchen table and raised their glasses full of creamy milk.

"Here's to a breakfast for growing boys," joked Victor Kray, pretending to be starving as he attacked his first slice of toast.

Roland looked down.

"I was in the ship yesterday," he mumbled.

"I know," his grandfather replied, his mouth full. "Did you see anything new?"

Roland hesitated, then put the glass on the table and looked up at the old man, who was trying to maintain a cheerful expression.

"I think something bad is happening, Granddad," he said at last. "Something to do with some statues..."

Victor Kray felt his stomach lurch. He stopped chewing and put down his half-eaten piece of toast.

"This friend of mine, Max, he's seen things," Roland continued.

"Where does your friend live?" asked the old man calmly.

"In the Fleischmanns' old house, by the north beach."

Victor Kray nodded slowly.

"Roland, tell me everything you and your friends have seen. Please."

So Roland told him what had happened over the last two days, from the moment he had met Max to the events of the previous night.

When he finished his story, he glanced at his grandfather, trying to guess his thoughts. The old man gave him a reassuring smile but remained impassive.

"Finish your breakfast, Roland," he told him.

"But..." the boy protested.

"When you've finished, go and find your friends and bring them here," the old man continued. "We have a lot to talk about."

◆ ◆ ◆

That morning, at thirty-four minutes past eleven, Maximilian Carver phoned from the hospital to give his children the latest news. Irina was continuing to make progress, albeit slowly, but the doctors still couldn't assure them that she was out of danger. Alicia noticed that her father's voice seemed fairly calm, and so she guessed that the worst was over.

Five minutes later, the telephone rang again. This time it was Roland, calling from a café in town. They would meet at noon by the lighthouse. When Alicia put down the phone, she remembered the way Roland had looked at her, entranced, the night before on the beach. Smiling to herself, she went out to the porch to give Max the news. She recognized the outline of her brother, sitting on the beach, gazing out at the sea. Over the horizon, the first sparks of an electric storm crackled across the sky like a string of bright lights. Alicia walked down to the shore and sat next to Max. It was a cold morning and there was a bite in the air — she wished she'd brought a sweater with her.

"Roland called," she said. "His grandfather wants to see us."

Max didn't reply, his eyes still fixed on the sea. A flash of lightning tore through the sky.

"You like Roland, don't you?" Max asked, playing with a handful of sand, letting it trickle through his fingers.

Alicia considered her brother's question.

"Yes," she replied. "And I think he likes me, too. Why do you ask, Max?"

Max shrugged and threw the handful of sand toward the water's edge.

"I don't know. I was thinking about what Roland said,

about the war and all that. That he might be called up after the summer...It doesn't matter. I suppose it's none of my business."

Alicia turned to her younger brother and tried to look him in the eye. He raised his eyebrows the same way Maximilian Carver did, and she saw the reflections in his gray eyes, the bundle of nerves buried just beneath the surface of his skin.

Alicia put her arm round Max and kissed him on the cheek.

"Let's go in," she said, shaking off the sand that had stuck to her dress. "It's cold out here."

9

By the time they'd reached the path that led up to the lighthouse, Max felt as if his legs had turned to butter. Before setting off, Alicia had offered to take the other bicycle that lay dormant among the shadows of the garden shed, but Max had rejected the idea: He would take her on his bike just as Roland had done the day before. A kilometer farther on, he was already regretting his decision.

As if he'd guessed how painfully difficult the long ride would be, Roland was waiting with his bicycle at the foot of the path. When he saw him, Max stopped pedaling and let his sister off. He took a deep breath and rubbed his muscles, which were in agony.

"You look like you've shrunk a few centimeters, city boy," said Roland.

Max decided not to waste his breath responding to the joke. Without saying a word, Alicia climbed onto Roland's bike and they started up the hill. Max waited a few seconds before pushing off. He knew what he was going to spend his first paycheck on: a motorbike.

◆ ◆ ◆

The small dining room in the lighthouse cottage smelled of freshly brewed coffee and pipe tobacco. The floor and the walls were lined with dark wood and, apart from a very large bookcase and a few nautical objects that Max was unable to identify, there was barely any other decoration. A wood-burning stove and a table covered with a dark velvet cloth, surrounded by old armchairs of faded leather, were the only luxuries Victor Kray had allowed himself.

Roland asked his friends to sit in the armchairs while he sat on a wooden chair between them. They waited for about five minutes, hardly speaking, listening to the old man's footsteps on the floor above.

At last, the lighthouse keeper made his appearance. He wasn't as Max had imagined him. Victor Kray was a man of average height, with pale skin and a generous head of silvery hair crowning a face that did not reflect his real age.

His green, penetrating eyes slowly scanned the faces of the brother and sister, as if he were trying to read their thoughts. Max smiled nervously and Victor Kray smiled back at him, the kind smile lighting up his face.

"You're the first visitors I've had in years," said the lighthouse keeper, taking a seat on one of the armchairs. "You'll have to forgive my manners. Anyhow, when I was a child, I thought all this business about the polite way of doing things was a lot of nonsense. I still do."

"We're not children, Granddad," said Roland.

"Anyone younger than me is a baby," replied Victor Kray. "You must be Alicia. And you're Max. You don't need much of a brain to work that out."

Alicia smiled warmly. She'd known the old man for only a couple of minutes, but already she was charmed by the way he put them at ease. Max, meanwhile, was studying Victor's face and trying to imagine him shut away in that lighthouse for decades, guarding the secret of the *Orpheus*.

"I know what you must be thinking," Victor Kray continued. "Is everything we've seen or thought we've seen during these last couple of days real—is it true? To be honest, I never imagined the day would come when I'd have to talk about this to anyone, not even Roland.

But things often turn out differently from the way we expect. Don't you agree?"

Nobody replied.

"Right. Let's get straight to the point. First of all, you must tell me everything you know. And when I say everything, I mean *everything*. Including details that might seem insignificant to you. Everything. Do you understand?"

Max looked at the others.

"Shall I go first?"

Alicia and Roland nodded. Victor Kray gestured to him to begin his story.

♦ ♦ ♦

During the next half hour, Max recounted everything he remembered, without a pause. The eyes of the old man were attentive as he listened to Max's words without the slightest hint of disbelief or—as Max was expecting—of surprise.

When Max had finished his story, Victor Kray took out his pipe and began to pack it with tobacco.

"Not bad," he muttered, "not bad..."

The lighthouse keeper lit his pipe and a cloud of sweet-smelling smoke enveloped the room. He took a few puffs of his special tobacco and sat back in his armchair. Then, looking the three friends in the eye, he began to speak.

◆ ◆ ◆

"I'll be seventy-two this autumn and although people say I don't look my age, every year weighs on my back like a tombstone. Age makes you notice certain things. For example, I now know that a man's life is broadly divided into three periods. During the first, it doesn't even occur to us that one day we will grow old, we don't think that time passes or that from the day we are born we're all walking toward a common end. After the first years of youth comes the second period, in which a person becomes aware of the fragility of life and what begins like a simple niggling doubt rises inside you like a flood of uncertainties that will stay with you for the rest of your days. Finally, toward the end of life, we reach the period of acceptance and, consequently, of resignation—a time of waiting. Throughout my life I've known quite a few people who have become trapped in one of these stages and have never managed to get beyond them. It's a terrible thing."

Victor Kray noticed they were listening intently, but they seemed to be slightly puzzled, wondering where he was going with all this. He stopped to enjoy another puff of his pipe and beamed at his audience.

"This is a path we must all learn to follow on our own, praying we won't lose our way before reaching the end.

If at the beginning of our lives we were able to understand this apparently simple fact, we would be spared many of the miseries and pains of this world. But—and this is one of the great paradoxes of the universe—we are only granted this knowledge when it is already too late. Here endeth the lesson.

"You'll wonder why I'm telling you all this. Let me explain. One time in a million, someone who is still very young understands that life is a one-way journey and he decides that the rules of the game don't agree with him. It's like when you decide to cheat because you know you can't win. Usually you're found out and you can't cheat anymore. But sometimes, the cheater gets away with it. And if, instead of playing with dice or cards, the game consists of playing with life and death, then the cheater turns into someone very dangerous indeed.

"A long time ago, when I was your age, one of the greatest cheaters that have ever set foot on this earth happened to cross my path. I never discovered his real name. In the poor area where I lived, all the kids on the street knew him as Cain. Others called him the Prince of Mist, because, as rumor had it, he always appeared out of the thick haze that covered the streets and alleyways at night, and before dawn he disappeared again into the shadows.

"Cain was a good-looking young man, but nobody seemed to know where he'd come from. Every night, in one of the many alleyways of our area, he would gather the local youngsters together—all of them ragged and covered in grime and soot from the factories—and he would propose a pact. Each child could make a wish and Cain would make it come true. In exchange, he asked for one thing only: complete loyalty. One night Angus, my best friend, took me to one of Cain's meetings. Cain was dressed like a gentleman who'd come straight from the opera, and he never stopped smiling. His eyes seemed to change color in the dark and his voice was deep and measured. According to the other boys, Cain was a magician. I hadn't believed a single word of the stories circulating about him, and that night I went along, fully intending to have a laugh at this supposed magician. And yet I remember that, in his presence, any desire to make fun of him immediately vanished into thin air. As soon as I saw him, the only emotion I felt was fear and I was careful not to open my mouth. That night a few of the lads from the street made their wishes known to Cain. When they'd finished, Cain turned his icy eyes to the corner where my friend Angus and I were standing. He asked us whether we had any requests. I stood there, trying to keep my expression blank, but to my surprise, Angus spoke. His father had lost his job that day. The steel plant where most of the local adults worked was laying off a substantial part of the workforce and replacing it with machines that worked longer hours for no pay and didn't complain. The first people to lose their jobs in this lottery were the more troublesome leaders, and Angus's father seemed to meet all the requirements.

"Angus had five brothers and sisters and his mother was sick, barely able to leave her bed. They all lived together squeezed into a miserable damp house that was falling to pieces. I don't need to tell you the situation was desperate. In a small voice, Angus made his wish known to Cain: that his father get his job back at the steelworks. Cain agreed and then, just as I had been told, we saw him disappear off into the mist. The following day, Angus's father was inexplicably called back to work. Cain had fulfilled his promise.

"Two weeks later, Angus and I were returning home after a visit to a traveling fair on the outskirts of town. We didn't want to get back too late, so we took a shortcut along an abandoned railway line. It was dark, and as we were walking through that eerie, moonlit landscape, we saw a figure emerging from the mist and coming toward us. The figure was wrapped in a dark cloak. The Prince of Mist. We were paralyzed with fear. Cain approached us and, with his usual smile, he spoke to Angus. He told my friend that the time had come for him to return the favor. Stricken with terror, Angus agreed. Cain said that his request was a simple one: a small settling of scores. In those days, the richest person in the area, in fact, the only rich person, was Skolimoski, a Polish tradesman who owned a food and clothing store where everyone did their shopping. Angus's mission was to set fire to Skolimoski's shop. The task was to be completed the following night. Angus tried to protest, but he couldn't get the words out. There was something in Cain's eyes that made it clear he was not prepared to accept anything other than total obedience. The magician left the same way he'd come.

"We ran all the way home, and when I left Angus at his door and saw the horror that filled his eyes, my heart went out to him. The following day I combed the streets looking for my friend, but there was no trace of him. I was beginning to worry that Angus had decided to carry out the criminal act requested by Cain, so I decided to stand guard opposite Skolimoski's store as soon as it grew dark. Angus never turned up, and the Pole's shop didn't go up in flames that night. I felt guilty for having doubted my friend and thought the best thing I could do was try to reassure him. I knew him well; he was bound to be at home, hiding, trembling at the thought of the sinister magician's revenge. The next morning I went to his house. Angus wasn't there. With tears in her eyes, his mother told me he hadn't come home that night and begged me to find him and bring him back.

"Sick with fear, I scoured the whole area from top to

bottom, not forgetting a single one of its stinking corners. Nobody had seen him. By the evening, exhausted and not knowing where else I could possibly look, a dark thought took hold of me. I returned to the path by the old railway line and followed the tracks that glowed faintly in the moonlight. I didn't have to walk for long. I found my friend lying on the rails, in the same place where Cain had appeared out of the mist two nights before. I tried to feel his pulse, but my hands could find no skin on that body. Only ice. The body of my friend had been transformed into a grotesque statue of smoking blue ice that was slowly melting onto the abandoned line. Around his neck was a small medal with the same symbol I remembered seeing stamped on Cain's cloak—a six-pointed star within a circle. I stayed with Angus until his features vanished forever into the gloom in a pool of cold tears.

"That same night, while I discovered my friend's horrific fate, Skolimoski's store was destroyed by a ferocious fire. I never told anybody what I had witnessed that day.

"Two months later, my family moved south, to a place far from our old home. As the months went by I started to believe that the Prince of Mist was only a bitter memory, a fragment of the bleak years spent in the shadows of that poor, dirty, violent town of my childhood...until I saw him again and realized that what had happened that night had been only the beginning."

10

MY NEXT ENCOUNTER with the Prince of Mist took place a few months later. My father had just been promoted to chief engineer in a textile factory, and to celebrate he decided to take us all to a large amusement park built on a wooden pier. I'll never forget it. The pier stretched out into the sea and the buildings on it shone like a glass palace suspended from the sky. When night fell, the sight of all the multicolored lights reflected on the water was magnificent. I'd never seen anything so beautiful. My father was over the moon: He'd rescued his family from what had promised to be a miserable future and was now a man with a good job, was highly regarded, and had enough money in his pocket to be able to let his children enjoy the same amusements as any other child in town. We had an early dinner and then my father gave us each a few coins to spend on whatever we liked, while he and my mother strolled about arm in arm, rubbing shoulders with the well-to-do.

"I was fascinated by the Big Wheel that turned cease-lessly at one end of the pier—its lights could be seen for miles along the coast—and I ran to join the queue. While I waited I became aware of a booth standing only a few meters away. Between lucky dips and shooting gal-leries, an intense purple light illuminated the mysterious den of Dr. Cain, fortune-teller, magician, and clairvoy-ant, as the notice outside proclaimed. A third-rate art-ist had depicted Cain's face on the sign; his eyes stared threateningly at any onlookers who walked over to the new lair of the Prince of Mist. The portrait, together with the shadows projected by the purple lamp, lent the den a chilling, funereal appearance. A curtain with the six-pointed star embroidered in black cloaked the entrance.

"As if drawn by an invisible force, I left the queue for the Big Wheel and walked over to the hut. I was trying to peek inside through a narrow gap when the curtain was flung open and a woman dressed in black, with snow-white skin and dark, piercing eyes, beckoned to me. Inside, sit-ting behind a table under the glow of an oil lamp, was the man I had met in another place and time: Cain. A large, dark cat with golden eyes was grooming itself at his feet.

"Without thinking twice, I went over to the table where the Prince of Mist was waiting for me, a smile on his face. I still remember his voice, deep and measured, saying my name over the hypnotic sound of the music from a merry-go-round that seemed to be far, far away...."

◆ ◆ ◆

"Victor, my friend," Cain murmured. "If I weren't a fortune-teller I'd say that fate wished our paths to cross again."

"Who *are* you?" young Victor managed to stammer as he glanced over at the ghostly woman who had retreated into the shadows.

"I'm Dr. Cain. Surely you saw the sign?" Cain replied. "Having a nice time with your family?"

Victor gulped and nodded.

"That's good," the magician went on. "Amusement is like laudanum; it takes away all the misery and pain, even if only for a short time."

"I don't know what laudanum is," replied Victor.

"A drug, my son, it's a drug," Cain replied wearily, turning to look at a clock resting on a shelf to his right.

The hands seemed to be going backward.

"Time does not exist; that's why we mustn't lose it. Have you decided on your wish?"

"I don't have a wish," Victor replied shakily.

Cain burst out laughing.

"Come, come. None of us has only one wish, we have hundreds. And life doesn't grant us many chances to make them come true." Cain looked over at the mysterious woman with a grimace that was meant to look like pity. "Isn't that true, dearest?"

The woman didn't reply. It almost seemed as if she was made of wood and was incapable of movement.

"But some of us are lucky, Victor," said Cain, leaning over the table. "Like you. Because you can make your dreams come true, Victor. And you know how."

"The way Angus did?" Victor snapped despite himself. He'd noticed something odd that he couldn't get out of his mind: Cain hadn't blinked at all, not even once.

"An accident, dear friend. An unfortunate accident," said Cain, adopting a note of concern. "It's a mistake to think that dreams can come true without having to offer anything in exchange. Don't you agree, Victor? It wouldn't be fair. Angus tried to forget he had certain obligations and that could not be tolerated. But that is all in the past. Let's talk about the future, your future."

"Is that what *you* did?" Victor asked, emboldened by fear. "Make your own dream come true? To become what you are now? What did *you* have to give in exchange?"

Cain lost his reptilian smile and fixed his eyes on Victor Kray. For a moment the boy feared Cain was going to

111

pounce on him and tear him to shreds. Eventually, Cain sighed.

"An intelligent young man. That's what I like, Victor. And yet you still have a lot to learn. When you're ready, come and visit me again. You'll know how to find me. I hope to see you soon."

"I doubt it," Victor replied, getting to his feet, his heart still pounding.

Like a sagging puppet whose strings have suddenly been pulled, the woman started to walk toward him, as if to see him out. Victor was only a few steps from the door when he heard Cain's voice behind him.

"One more thing, Victor. About your wishes. Give it some thought. The offer still stands. You may not be interested, but perhaps some member of your wonder-fully happy family has a secret desire they dare not men-tion. That's my specialty...."

Without pausing to reply, Victor stepped out into the fresh night air. He took a deep breath and ran off in search of his family. As he left, Dr. Cain's laughter echoed behind him like the cry of a hyena.

◆ ◆ ◆

Until then, Max had been listening spellbound to the old man's story, without daring to ask any of the thousands of questions that were spilling over in his brain. Victor Kray seemed to read his thoughts and pointed at him accusingly.

"Patience, young man. All the pieces will fit together in due course. You're not allowed to interrupt. Okay?"

Although the warning was directed at Max, the friends agreed in unison.

"Good, good..." the lighthouse keeper mumbled.

♦ ♦ ♦

"That night I decided to stay away from that man forever and try to erase any thoughts about him from my mind. It wasn't easy. Whoever Dr. Cain was, he had a strange way of getting inside your head, like a splinter that goes deeper into your skin the more you try to pull it out. I couldn't talk about him with anyone or they'd think I was a lunatic, and I couldn't go to the authorities because I wouldn't have known where to begin. So I did the only thing that seemed wise in this sort of situation: I decided to let time go by.

"Things were going well for us in our new home and I was lucky enough to meet someone who proved to be a great help to me: a priest who taught math and physics at school. His name was Darius. At first he seemed to have his head in the clouds half the time, but, in fact, his intelligence was equaled only by his kindness, although he concealed it well, pretending to be just another mad scientist. Darius encouraged me to work hard and discover the joys of mathematics, so it wasn't surprising that, after a few years in his charge, my talent for science became increasingly clear. Initially, I wanted to follow in his footsteps and devote myself to teaching, but the reverend father gave me a severe lecture and said that what I had to do was go to college, study physics, and become the best engineer the country had ever seen. Either I did that, or he would never speak to me again.

"Darius was the one who managed to get me a university grant and who set me on the path toward what could, or should, have been. He passed away the week before my graduation. I'm no longer ashamed to say that I felt his loss as much, or more, than the loss of my own father. In college I became a close friend of the person who would lead me once more to a meeting with Dr. Cain: a young medical student whose family was scandalously wealthy—or so it seemed to me—named Richard Fleischmann. Indeed, the future Dr. Fleischmann who, years later, would build the house by the beach.

"Richard Fleischmann was an impetuous young man, prone to excess. He was used to the fact that throughout his life things had always turned out the way he'd wanted them to and when, for any reason, something did not go as planned he would fly into a rage. A quirk of fate is what led us to become friends: We both fell in love with the same woman, Eva Gray, the daughter of the most unbearable, tyrannical chemistry professor on campus.

"At first, we'd all go out together, the three of us, and on Sundays we'd go away for the day, whenever that ogre, Theodore Gray, didn't manage to stop us. But this arrangement didn't last long. The most curious thing about it was that Fleischmann and I, far from becoming rivals, became the best of friends. Every night, when we returned Eva to the ogre's cave, we'd walk back to our rooms together knowing that, sooner or later, one of us would be out of the running.

"Until that day came, we spent the best two years of my life together. But everything must come to an end. The breakdown of our inseparable trio arrived on the night of our graduation. Although I'd achieved every kind of success imaginable, I was feeling down in the dumps because of the death of my old tutor. So, although I never drank, Eva and Richard decided they should get me drunk that night to rid me of my melancholy. Needless to say, Professor Theodore, who supposedly was as deaf as a post yet seemed to be able to hear through walls when it suited him, uncovered our plan, and when the evening ended, Fleischmann and I found ourselves alone, completely smashed in some seedy bar, where we devoted our time to praising the object of our impossible love, Eva Gray.

"That same night, as we stumbled back to the campus, a traveling fair seemed to emerge from the mist beside the railway station. Convinced that a ride on the merry-go-round would cure us of our drunken state, Fleischmann and I walked into the fair and ended up outside the den of Dr. Cain, magician, fortune-teller, and clairvoyant, as his sinister sign still announced. Fleischmann had a brilliant idea. We would go in and ask the fortune-teller to reveal the enigma: Which of us would Eva choose? Despite my drunken daze, I had enough common sense not to go in, but I could not stop my friend, who rushed headlong into the tent.

"I suppose I passed out, because I don't remember much about the following hours. When I regained consciousness, my head throbbing, Fleischmann and I were lying on an old wooden bench. Day was breaking and the caravans from the fair had disappeared, as if all the lights, noise, and crowds of the night had been an illusion conjured by our alcohol-soaked brains. We stood up and gazed at the deserted plot of land around us. I asked my friend whether he remembered anything about the previous night. Fleischmann told me he'd dreamed that he'd gone into a magician's den, and when he'd been asked what his greatest wish was, he'd replied that he wanted to be loved by Eva Gray. Then he laughed, joking about our monumental hangover, convinced that nothing he'd told me had actually happened.

"Two months later, Eva Gray and Richard Fleischmann were married. They didn't even invite me to the wedding. I wouldn't see them again for over twenty years."

◆ ◆ ◆

"One wet winter's day, a man wearing a raincoat followed me from the office to my home. From the dining room window I could see that the stranger was still down there, watching my house. I hesitated for a few moments and then went outside, ready to unmask the mysterious spy. It was Richard Fleischmann, trembling with cold, his face wrinkled with age and a haunted look in his eyes. My old friend looked as if he hadn't slept in months. I made him come in and offered him a cup of hot coffee. Without daring to look me in the eye he asked about that night long ago, in Dr. Cain's lair.

"I was in no mood for pleasantries. I asked him what Cain had demanded in exchange for making his wish come true. Fleischmann, his face distorted by fear and shame, sank to his knees in front of me, crying and begging for my help. I ignored his tears, insisting on an answer to my question. What had he promised Dr. Cain in exchange for his services?

"'My first-born son,' he replied. 'I promised him my son.'"

◆ ◆ ◆

"Fleischmann confessed to me that for years, and without her knowledge, he'd been administering a drug to his wife that prevented her from conceiving a child. But eventually Eva Fleischmann had plunged into a deep depression, and the absence of the child she so desired had turned their marriage into a living hell. Fleischmann was afraid that if Eva didn't conceive she would soon lose her mind, or that, with so much sadness, her life would slowly be extinguished, like a candle going out through lack of oxygen. He told me there was no one else he could turn to and he begged my forgiveness, then asked for my help. In the end, I said I would help him, not for his sake but out of the affection I still felt for Eva Gray and in memory of our old friendship.

"That very night I threw Fleischmann out of my house, but my plan was very different from what the man I had once considered my friend imagined. I followed him through the rain, tracking him across the city. I asked myself why I was doing it. But the very thought that Eva

Gray, who had rejected me when we were both so young, might have to hand over her son to that vile sorcerer made my stomach turn and was sufficient reason for me to confront Dr. Cain once more, even though I was increasingly aware that I might not escape unharmed.

"Fleischmann's ramblings led me to the new lair of my former acquaintance, the Prince of Mist. His new home was a traveling circus and, to my surprise, Dr. Cain had given up his role as fortune-teller and clairvoyant in favor of a persona more in keeping with his sense of humor. He was dressed as a clown, his face painted white and red, although his constantly changing eyes gave away his identity even beneath dozens of layers of makeup. Cain's circus flew a flag decorated with the six-pointed star at the top of a tall mast, and the magician had surrounded himself with a group of sinister companions who used the cover of being circus performers to disguise something else, much darker. For two weeks I spied on Cain's circus and soon discovered that its threadbare, yellowing big top concealed a gang of tricksters, criminals, and thieves who robbed and stole wherever they went. I also discovered that Dr. Cain's lack of care in choosing his slaves had resulted in a trail of crimes, disappearances, and thefts that had not gone unnoticed by the local police, who could smell the stench of corruption emanating from the ghoulish troupe.

"Naturally, Cain was aware of the situation, so he decided that he and his friends must vanish from the country as quickly as possible, but in a discreet way, preferably avoiding the police and their irritating procedures. That is how, taking advantage of a gambling debt that had been handed to him at a convenient moment—thanks to the stupidity of the Dutch captain—Dr. Cain was able to board the *Orpheus* that night. And I alongside him.

"What happened on the night of the storm is something that even I cannot explain. Fierce winds dragged the *Orpheus* toward the coast and flung her against the rocks, opening a gash in the hull that caused her to sink in a matter of minutes. I was hiding in one of the lifeboats, which had broken loose when the ship ran aground and was then hurled by the breakers onto the beach. That is the only reason I survived. Cain and his henchmen were traveling in the bilge, hidden under crates in case of a military inspection halfway through the journey. I suppose that when the icy water flooded the bowels of the ship, they didn't even realize what was happening...."

◆ ◆ ◆

"And the bodies were never found." Max was stunned.

Victor Kray shook his head.

"Often, when storms are violent, the sea carries the bodies away," said the lighthouse keeper.

"But it usually returns them, even if it's many days later," Max replied. "I've read that."

"Don't believe everything you read," said the old man, "although in this case it could be true."

"Then what happened?" asked Alicia.

"For years I've had a theory even I didn't quite believe. But now everything seems to confirm it."

◆ ◆ ◆

"I was the sole survivor of the shipwreck. Yet when I recovered consciousness in the hospital I realized that something strange had occurred. I decided to build this lighthouse and stay here, but you already know that part of the story. I was sure that the night of the storm didn't spell the end of Dr. Cain; it was only a pause in time. That's why I've remained here all these years. When Roland's parents died some time later, I took him in and he, in exchange, has been my only companion during my exile.

"But that isn't all. A few years later I made another fatal mistake. I tried to get in touch with Eva Gray. I suppose I wanted to know if everything I'd gone through had been worth it. Fleischmann got to it first—he discovered my whereabouts and paid me a visit. I told him what had happened, and my words seemed to free him of all the ghosts that had tormented him for years. He decided to build the house by the beach and, soon after, little Jacob was born. Those were the best years of Eva's life. Until the death of the boy.

"The day Jacob Fleischmann drowned I knew that the Prince of Mist had never left. He had remained in the shadows, waiting patiently for something powerful to return him to the world of the living. And nothing is as powerful as a promise...."

11

WHEN THE OLD LIGHTHOUSE KEEPER finished his story, Max looked at his watch: It was a few minutes to five. Outside, light rain had started to fall across the bay and the wind from the sea banged insistently against the shutters.

"There's a storm brewing," said Roland, scanning the leaden horizon.

"Max, we should get back home. Dad is going to call us soon," Alicia added.

Max agreed, reluctantly. He needed to consider everything the old man had told them, to try to fit the pieces of the jigsaw together. The effort of remembering his tale seemed to have plunged Victor Kray into a listless silence, and he stared blankly ahead from his armchair.

"Max..." Alicia hissed.

Max stood up and waved a silent good-bye to the old man, who responded with a tiny nod of his head. Roland observed the old lighthouse keeper for a few seconds more, then followed his friends outside.

"What now?" asked Max.

"I don't know what to think," Alicia declared.

"Don't you believe the story?" asked Max.

"It's not an easy story to believe," Alicia replied. "There must be some other explanation."

Max looked at Roland.

"You don't believe your grandfather either, Roland?"

"Honestly, I don't know what to believe....Anyway, let's go before the storm reaches us. I'll come with you."

Alicia jumped onto Roland's bicycle and they sped off on the return journey. Max turned for a moment to look at the cottage and wondered whether years of solitude on the cliff top could have led Victor Kray to make up his grim story, which he clearly believed to be true. He let the cool drizzle refresh his face then set off downhill.

The tale of Cain and Victor Kray was still running through his mind when he reached the road that bordered the bay. Riding on through the rain, Max began to sort the facts into the only order that seemed plausible to him. Even supposing that everything the old man had told them was true—which was hard to accept—the situation was still unclear. A powerful magician who had been hibernating for many years appeared to be slowly coming back to life. If he followed this train of thought, the death of Jacob Fleischmann had been the first sign of Cain's return. And yet there was something about the whole story, which the lighthouse keeper had concealed for so long, that just didn't add up.

The first flashes of lightning stained the sky scarlet, and the strong wind began to spit large drops of rain in Max's face. He hurried on, even though his legs had not yet recovered from that morning's exercise. There were still a couple of kilometers to go before he reached the beach house.

Max knew he couldn't simply accept the old man's tale and assume that it explained everything. The ghostly presence of the statues in the walled garden and the events of those first few days in the town suggested that some sinister mechanism had been set in motion and nobody could predict what might happen next. With or without the help of Roland and Alicia, Max was determined to carry on his investigation until he got to the bottom of the mystery. He would begin with something that could maybe hold the key to the whole conundrum: Jacob Fleischmann's films. The more he went over the story in his mind, the more Max was convinced that Victor Kray hadn't told them everything. Not by a long shot.

◆ ◆ ◆

Alicia and Roland were waiting on the porch when Max, soaking wet, left his bicycle in the shed and ran over to take shelter from the downpour.

"That's the second time this week," laughed Max. "At this rate I'll shrink. You're not thinking of going back now, are you Roland?"

"'Fraid so," he replied, gazing at the thick curtain of water. "I don't want to leave my grandfather alone."

"At least take a coat. You'll catch your death out there," Alicia pointed out.

"I don't need one, I'm used to it. Besides, it's only a summer storm. It'll soon be over."

"The voice of experience," joked Max.

"Well, yes..."

"I think we shouldn't talk about it anymore until tomorrow," Alicia suggested after a pause. "A good night's sleep will help us see things more clearly. That's what my father always says."

"And who's going to sleep tonight after a story like that?" Max blurted out.

"Your sister's right," said Roland.

"Take her side, why don't you?" Max shot back.

"Changing the subject, I was planning to go diving again tomorrow. I might get back the sextant someone dropped the other day...." Roland stated.

Max was trying to think of a crushing reply—he thought that it was a terrible idea to go diving around the *Orpheus* once more—but Alicia answered first.

"We'll be there," she said softly.

A sixth sense told Max that the plural she had used was just her way of being polite.

"I'll see you tomorrow then," Roland replied, his eyes never leaving Alicia's face.

"Hello, I'm here," said Max in a singsong voice.

"See you tomorrow, Max." Roland walked off toward his bicycle.

They watched as Roland rode off into the storm, remaining on the porch until his figure had disappeared.

"You should put on some dry clothes, Max. While you change I'll make something for dinner," Alicia said.

"You?" Max retorted. "You can't even cook."

"Who said anything about cooking? This isn't a hotel. In you go," ordered Alicia, a wicked smile on her lips.

Max decided to follow her advice and went indoors. The absence of Irina and his parents increased the feeling that he was an intruder in a stranger's home. It was unusually quiet inside, as if something was missing. As he climbed the stairs toward his bedroom, he realized what it was. The cat. He hadn't seen Irina's odious pet for a couple of days now. All things considered, he decided it wasn't a great loss and put the thought from his mind.

◆ ◆ ◆

True to her word, Alicia didn't waste a second longer in the kitchen than was strictly necessary. She prepared a few slices of bread with butter and jam and poured two glasses of milk.

When Max glimpsed the tray with what was supposed to be his dinner, the expression on his face said it all.

"Not one word," Alicia threatened. "I didn't come into this world to spend my life cooking."

"You don't say…" replied Max, who wasn't very hungry anyway.

They ate their meal quietly, waiting for the phone to ring with news from the hospital, but the call didn't come.

"Perhaps they rang earlier, while we were at the lighthouse," Max suggested.

"Perhaps," said Alicia.

Max noticed the worried expression on his sister's face.

"If anything had happened, they would have called," he argued. "Everything will be fine."

Alicia smiled in relief, confirming to Max his ability to comfort others with arguments that even he didn't believe.

"I suppose so," she agreed. "I'm going to bed. What about you?"

Max downed his milk and pointed toward the kitchen.

"I'll be up in a minute, but I think I'll get something else to eat. I'm starving," he lied.

"On you go. I'm done."

Max watched his sister disappear upstairs. As soon as he heard Alicia close her bedroom door, Max put down his glass and went off to the shed in search of more films from Jacob Fleischmann's private collection.

◆ ◆ ◆

Max turned on the projector and the beam of light flooded the wall with the blurred image of what looked like a collection of symbols. Slowly, the picture came into focus, and Max realized that what he'd thought were symbols were numbers placed in a circle and that he was looking at the face of a clock. The hands of the clock were still, and the shadows they projected onto the face were clear and defined, from which Max inferred that the shot was filmed in full sunlight or at least under an intense source of light. The film continued to show the clock face until, slowly at first and then progressively gathering speed, the hands began to turn counterclockwise. The person operating the camera took a step back, and it became clear that the clock was hanging from a chain. A further backward movement of a meter or so revealed that this chain was suspended from a white hand. The hand of a statue.

Max immediately recognized the walled garden that had already appeared in the first of Jacob Fleischmann's films that he'd viewed a couple of days ago. As before, the position of the statues was different from how Max remembered it. Now the camera began to move through the figures again, with no cuts or pauses, just as it had in the first film. Every two meters or so the lens closed in on the face of one of the statues. One by one, Max examined the frozen expressions of the circus troupe. He pictured them fighting in vain to escape their horrific deaths in the pitch dark and icy waters of the *Orpheus*'s hold.

Finally, almost in slow motion, the camera approached the figure marking the center of the six-pointed star. The clown. Dr. Cain. The Prince of Mist. At his feet, Max noticed the motionless shape of a cat stretching a sharp claw in the air. Max, who didn't recall having seen it when he visited the walled garden, would have bet his life that the uncanny likeness between this stone cat and the creature Irina had adopted at the station was no coincidence. As he stared at the images, with the rain pounding against the windowpanes as the storm moved inland, it was easy to believe the story the lighthouse keeper had told them that afternoon. The malevolent presence of the stone figures was enough to remove any doubt, however reasonable that doubt might have seemed in the light of day.

The camera now closed in on the clown's face, pausing only half a meter away and remaining there for a few seconds. Max checked the reel: The film was coming to an end. Suddenly, a movement on the screen caught his attention. The stone face was moving, almost imperceptibly. Max stood up and walked over to the wall on which the film was being projected. The pupils of those stone eyes dilated, and the lips arched slowly into a cruel smile, laying bare a row of long, sharp teeth, like the fangs of a wolf. Max felt his throat constrict.

An instant later, the image disappeared and Max heard the reel spinning as the film ended.

Max turned off the projector and took a deep breath. Now he believed everything Victor Kray had said, but this didn't make him feel any better—quite the opposite. He went up to his room and closed the door behind him. Through the window, in the distance, he could just about make out the walled garden. Once again, the stone enclosure was submerged in a dense, impenetrable mist.

That night, however, the darkness didn't seem to come from the forest, but from within himself. It was as if the mist were nothing other than the frozen breath of Dr. Cain, waiting with a smile for the moment of his return.

12

WHEN MAX AWOKE the following morning, his head felt like a bowl of jelly. From what he could see out of the window, the storm was gone and it promised to be a bright, sunny day. He sat up lazily and took his watch from the bedside table. The first thing he thought was that it wasn't working properly. But when he put it next to his ear, he realized that the mechanism was working fine: *He* was the one who'd lost his bearings. It was twelve noon.

He jumped out of bed and rushed downstairs. There was a note on the dining room table. He picked it up and read his sister's spidery writing:

Good morning, Sleeping Beauty,

By the time you read this I'll be on the beach with Roland. I've borrowed your bicycle, hope you don't mind. I see you went to the movies last night, so I didn't want to wake you. Dad called first thing and says they still don't know when they'll be able to come home. There's been no change in Irina, but the doctors say she'll probably be out of the coma in a few days. I convinced Dad not to worry about us (it wasn't easy).

By the way, there's nothing for breakfast.

We'll be on the beach. Sweet dreams...

Alicia

Max reread the note three times before leaving it on the table. He ran upstairs and hurriedly washed his face. Then he slipped on a pair of swimming shorts and a blue shirt and went out to the garden shed to find the other bicycle. By the time he got to the road that skirted the beach, his stomach was already screaming for its morning rations, so when he reached the town he changed direction and headed for the bakery in the main square. The delicious aroma called to him from several meters away, and the approving rumbles of his stomach confirmed that he'd made the right decision. Two sweet buns and two chocolate bars later, he set off for the beach with a saintly smile stamped on his face.

◆ ◆ ◆

Alicia's bicycle was leaning on its stand by the path that led to the beach and Roland's cabin. Max left his bicycle next to his sister's. Still the city boy, he decided that even if the town didn't seem like a haven for thieves, it wouldn't be a bad idea to buy a couple of padlocks. He stopped for a moment to look at the lighthouse on the cliff top and then began walking toward the beach. Shortly before he came to the end of the path between tall grasses that led to the bay, he stopped.

On the shore, about twenty meters from where Max was standing, Alicia was lying on the sand. Leaning over her was Roland, his fingertips slowly caressing the pale skin of her belly. He drew closer to Alicia and kissed her on the lips. Alicia rolled onto her side then climbed on top of Roland, her hands pinning his against the sand. On her lips was a smile Max had never seen before.

Max took a step or two back and hid among the grass, praying they hadn't seen him. He remained there, not moving, wondering what he should do next. Turn up, smiling like an idiot, and wish them a good morning? Or go off for a walk?

Max didn't consider himself a spy, but he couldn't resist the temptation to peek once more through the tall grass at his sister and Roland. He could hear their laughter and see that Roland's hands were moving shyly over Alicia's body. Exploring. From the way his hands were shaking, Max deduced that this was, if not the first time, then at most the second time Roland had found himself in such a momentous situation. He wondered whether it was also the first time for Alicia. He had to admit that he didn't know the answer. Although they'd spent their whole lives living under the same roof, Alicia had always been a mystery to him.

To see her lying there on the beach kissing Roland made him feel uneasy, and it wasn't something he'd expected. From the beginning he'd realized that there was something between her and Roland, but it was one thing to imagine it and another, very different thing to see it with his own eyes. He peered out again but suddenly felt that he had no right to be there: The moment belonged only to his sister and Roland. Silently he retraced his steps as far as the bicycles and left the beach.

As he did so he wondered whether perhaps he was jealous. Maybe it was just that he'd spent years thinking of his sister as a child, older than he was but with no secrets, certainly someone who didn't go around kissing people. For a moment he laughed at his own naïveté, and gradually he started to feel better about what he'd seen. He couldn't predict what would happen the following week, or what the end of the summer would bring, but that day Max was sure that his sister was happy. And that was more than he'd been able to say about her for many years.

Max rode back to the town center and left his bike by the library. Inside, he found an old glass counter displaying the library's opening hours and other public notices, including the monthly program for the only theater in the region, and a map of the town. Max concentrated on the map, studying it carefully. The layout looked very similar to the way he'd imagined it.

It was a detailed outline showing the port, the town center, the north beach where the Carvers' house was situated, the bay to the south with the *Orpheus* and the lighthouse, the park near the railway station, and the cemetery. A thought flashed through Max's mind. The local cemetery. Why hadn't he thought of it before? He looked at his watch and saw that it was already ten past two. Grabbing his bicycle, he rode off up the main street, heading for the road that led away from the shore, toward the small graveyard where he hoped to find the tomb of Jacob Fleischmann.

◆ ◆ ◆

The cemetery was a large rectangular enclosure, reached via a long path that wound its way uphill between tall cypress trees. There was nothing particularly original about it, he supposed. The stone walls seemed quite old, though not ancient, and from the outside it looked like the typical small-town graveyard where, except for a couple of days a year—excluding local funerals—visitors were few and far between. The gates were open and a metal sign, covered in rust, announced that the opening hours were from nine AM to five PM in the summer and from eight to four in winter. If anyone was guarding the place, Max couldn't tell.

On his way there, he had prepared himself for a somber, sinister landscape, but the bright early-summer sunshine made it look more like a cloister, quiet and only vaguely sad.

Max left his bicycle leaning against the outer wall and walked into the cemetery. It seemed to be dotted with modest tombstones that probably belonged to some of the more established local families. Here and there he saw walls containing recesses for burial urns that appeared to be more recent.

Although it had crossed his mind that the Fleischmanns might have preferred to bury their little Jacob far from this place, something told Max that the remains of Dr. Fleischmann's heir would be resting in the town in which he was born. It took him almost half an hour to find the grave, at the far end of the cemetery under the shade of two old cypress trees. It was a mausoleum to which time and rain had lent an air of abandon and neglect. The structure resembled a narrow marble hut, and it was blackened and dirty. Its wrought-iron gate was flanked by statues of two angels that looked toward heaven with imploring eyes. Jammed between the rusty bars of the gate was a bunch of dried flowers that must have been there since time immemorial.

An aura of sadness seemed to surround the tomb and, although it was obvious that it hadn't been visited for some time, the echoes of pain and tragedy still felt recent. He followed the flagstone path leading up to the tomb and stopped at the entrance. The gate was half open and a strong smell of musty air came from within. All around, there was complete silence. Max glanced one last time at the stone angels guarding Jacob Fleischmann's tomb and entered, aware that if he waited one more minute, he'd be tempted to run away from the place as fast as his legs could carry him.

The inside of the mausoleum was engulfed in darkness. Max was able to make out a trail of dead flowers on the floor, leading to the foot of a tombstone on which Jacob Fleischmann's name had been carved. But there was something else. Under Jacob's name, presiding over the stone that held his remains, was the symbol of a six-pointed star within a circle.

Max felt an unpleasant tingling down his spine, and for the first time, he wondered why he'd come to the cemetery on his own. Behind him, the daylight seemed to be growing fainter. He pulled out his watch and looked at the time, thinking that perhaps he'd spent longer in this place than he'd intended and that some guard had locked the gates, leaving him trapped inside. The hands on his watch showed it was two minutes past three. Max took a deep breath and tried to calm down.

He had a last look around, and after making sure there was nothing else here that could shed new light on the story of Dr. Cain, he got ready to leave. It was then that he realized he was not alone inside the tomb. He could hear the sound behind him. A sound like nails clicking over stone. He slowly turned around; something was moving in the gloom, a dark figure creeping along the ceiling, advancing slowly, like an insect. Max broke out in a cold sweat and he could feel his watch slipping from his hands. He took a few steps back and looked up. At first he could only make out the eyes, which were trained on him. One of the stone angels he'd seen at the entrance was walking upside down on the ceiling. The figure stopped and, staring at Max, gave a canine smile, then pointed an accusing finger at him. Gradually, the angel's features melted until they were transformed into the familiar face of the clown, Dr. Cain. Max could see burning anger and hatred in those eyes. He knew he had to run to the door but his legs wouldn't respond. Terrified, he could only close his eyes and stand, rooted to the spot, shaking, waiting for those stone claws to caress his face. Moments later, he felt a fetid, icy breath on his cheek. He opened his eyes, resolved to face death head on, but there was nothing there. The apparition had dissolved into the shadows. Max still stood, paralyzed. Perhaps the creature was just behind his back, closing in.

This time he didn't hang around. He ran to the exit as fast as he could and didn't stop to look behind him until he was back on his bike and had put at least a hundred meters between himself and the cemetery gates. Pedaling furiously helped him to regain control of his nerves. He told himself it had just been a trick of the light, a macabre manipulation of his own fears. That was all. Maybe there was still time for him to go back to the beach and join his sister and Roland for a swim. He was about to check his watch when he realized it wasn't there. He'd dropped the precious present his father had given him for his birthday inside the tomb.

"You idiot," he muttered to himself.

He contemplated his options. The idea of returning to that place to recover his watch was unthinkable.

Defeated, Max rode back toward the bay. But this time he wasn't looking for Roland and his sister; he wanted to see the old lighthouse keeper. There were a number of questions he wanted to ask the old man.

◆ ◆ ◆

The lighthouse keeper listened attentively to Max's account of what had happened in the cemetery. When the story was over, he nodded gravely and gestured to Max to sit down next to him.

"Can I be honest with you, Mr. Kray?" Max asked.

"I hope you will be, young man," Victor Kray replied. "When you get to my age you realize lying is a waste of time."

"But you lied to us, sir," Max said, instantly regretting his bluntness.

Victor Kray regarded him with piercing eyes. "What makes you think I did, Max?"

Max tried to choose his words more carefully this time. He had not meant to offend the lighthouse keeper and was convinced that if the old man had not told them the whole truth it was probably for a reason.

"I have a feeling that yesterday you didn't tell us everything you know. Don't ask me why—it's just a hunch," said Max.

"A hunch," echoed Victor Kray.

"My father says a hunch is your brain's way of taking a shortcut to the truth," replied Max.

"He's a wise man, your father. What else does he say?"

"That the more you try to hide from the truth, the quicker it finds you."

The lighthouse keeper smiled.

"And what do you think the truth is, Max?"

"I don't know.... I think that Dr. Cain, or whoever he is, is about to make a move. Soon," Max said. "And I think that all the things that have been happening over the last few days are just a sign of what is to come."

"What is to come," the lighthouse keeper repeated. "That's an interesting way of putting it, Max."

"Look, Mr. Kray," Max interjected. "I've had the fright of my life. Very strange things have been happening to me, and I'm sure my family, you, Roland, and I are in danger. The last thing I need right now is another mystery."

The old man smiled again, nodding.

"That's what I like. Direct and forceful." Victor Kray laughed without conviction. "You see, Max, if I told you the story about Dr. Cain yesterday, it wasn't to entertain you or to reminisce over old times. I told you so that you would all know what is happening and you'd be vigilant.

The last few days have been tough for you; I've been in this lighthouse for twenty-five years with one sole objective: to keep an eye on that beast. That's my only purpose in life. I'll be honest, too, Max. I'm not going to throw away twenty-five years because some kid decides to play detective. Maybe I shouldn't have told you anything. Perhaps it would be best if you forgot everything I've said and kept away from those statues and my grandson."

Max tried to protest, but the lighthouse keeper raised his hand and silenced him.

"I've already told you more than you need to know," Victor Kray pronounced. "Don't push it too far, Max. Forget Jacob Fleischmann and burn those films immediately. Today. That's the best advice I can give you. And now, young man, get out of here."

◆ ◆ ◆

Victor Kray watched Max cycle away. He knew he had been harsh and unfair to the boy, but in his heart he believed it was the wisest thing to do. He also knew that the lad was intelligent and he couldn't fool him. Max suspected that he was hiding something, but even so, he hadn't been able to grasp the magnitude of Victor's secret. Events were gathering pace and now, after a quarter of a century, as his life was nearing an end, Victor felt weaker and more alone than ever, his fear and anguish about the reappearance of Dr. Cain threatening to overwhelm him.

Victor Kray tried to banish the bitter memory of a whole existence entwined with that sinister character, from the dirty suburbs of his childhood to his imprisonment in the lighthouse. The Prince of Mist had robbed him of his best friend and of the only woman he had ever loved; he'd stolen every minute of his long adult life, turning him into his shadow. Victor Kray had spent countless nights in the lighthouse trying to imagine what his life might have been like if fate had not decided that the powerful magician would cross his path. Now he knew that any memories he might cherish during the last years of his life would be only fictions from a biography he'd never lived.

His last remaining hope lay in Roland and in the promise he'd made himself that the boy would have a future far away from that nightmare. There was little time left, and Victor's strength was nothing like the force that had once sustained him. In barely two days' time it would be exactly twenty-five years since the sinking of the *Orpheus*, and Victor Kray could sense that Cain was gathering power with every passing minute.

The old man went over to the window and gazed at the dark hulk of the *Orpheus* submerged beneath the blue waters of the bay. There were still a few hours of sunlight left before the darkness crept in and night fell—perhaps his last night of vigil in the lighthouse.

◆ ◆ ◆

When Max walked into the house by the beach, Alicia's note lay on the dining room table, which meant that his sister had not yet returned and was still with Roland. The empty house only intensified the loneliness Max felt at that moment. The old man's words echoed in his mind. Although he'd been hurt by the lighthouse keeper's tone, Max was not angry with him. He realized the old man was trying to protect them all from something that scared even him. Yet Max couldn't help shuddering, for what could be worse than what they already knew?

He went up to his room and lay on the bed, thinking that the entire story was beyond him and that, although he kept staring at the pieces of the puzzle, he couldn't find the right way to put them all together.

Perhaps he should follow Victor Kray's advice and forget the whole thing, even if it was only for a few hours. He looked at his bedside table and saw the neglected book on Copernicus still lying there, like an antidote to all the mysteries that surrounded him. He opened the book at the point where he'd left off and tried to concentrate on the rational arguments regarding the orbit of the planets. Maybe Copernicus would have been able to help him unravel the mystery, but the astronomer had clearly chosen the wrong time to alight in this world. In an infinite universe, there were too many things that escaped human understanding.

13

Hours later, when Max had eaten some food and was only ten pages away from the end of his book, he heard the sound of bicycles entering the front garden. Then came the soft hush of Roland's and Alicia's voices as they whispered for almost an hour on the porch. Around midnight, Max returned his book to the bedside table and turned off the lamp. Finally, he heard Roland's bike setting off down the road and Alicia tiptoeing up the stairs. His sister's footsteps paused for a moment outside his door, then continued along the short distance to her own bedroom. Max heard Alicia dropping her shoes on the wooden floor, then a creak as she lay down on the bed.

He recalled the image of Roland kissing her that morning on the beach, and he smiled in the dark. For once, he was certain that his sister would take much longer getting to sleep than he would.

◆ ◆ ◆

The following morning, Max decided to rise before the sun, and by dawn he was already cycling toward the bakery. He wanted to get something delicious for breakfast and prevent Alicia from preparing her specialty—leftovers of bread, jam, and milk. In the early hours, the town nestled in a calm that reminded him of Sunday mornings in the city. Only a few people out for a quiet walk broke the sleepy mood of the streets in which even the houses, their shutters closed, seemed to be dozing.

In the distance, beyond the harbor wall, the few fishing boats that made up the local fleet were gliding out to sea and would not return until sunset. Max was greeted by the baker and his daughter, a shy, young girl with rosy cheeks who stared at him as if he were some kind of prize. While they served him a mouth-watering tray of sweet cinnamon buns just out of the oven, the baker asked after Irina. Clearly the news had spread: The local doctor obviously did more than take his patients' temperatures when he made home visits. As his father liked to say, in small towns news traveled at the speed of boredom.

Max managed to get back to the beach house with the breakfast buns still irresistibly warm. Without his watch he wasn't sure what the time was, although he imagined it must be close to eight o'clock. The thought of having to wait for Alicia to wake up so he could have breakfast was not tempting, so he came up with a clever plan. With the excuse of giving her a hot breakfast, he prepared a tray with the pastries, milk, and a couple of napkins and went up to Alicia's bedroom. He rapped on the door with his knuckles until his sister's sleepy voice gave an unintelligible mumble.

"Room service," said Max. "Can I come in?"

He pushed the door open and stepped into the room. Alicia had buried her head under a pillow. Max looked around at the clothes hanging over chairs and her huge collection of random possessions. A girl's room was always a bewildering place, thought Max, a complete puzzle.

"I'll count to ten," he said, "then I'll start eating."

His sister's face peeped out from under the pillow just then, scenting the sweet aroma in the air.

◆ ◆ ◆

Roland was waiting for them by the edge of the beach, wearing just a pair of old trousers cut off at the knees. Next to him was a small boat that couldn't have been more than three meters long and looked as if it had spent at least thirty years bleaching in the sun; the wood had acquired a grayish hue, visible under the few remaining smudges of blue paint. Despite all that, Roland seemed to be admiring his boat as if it were a luxury yacht. And while Max and his sister walked down toward the shore, negotiating the stones on the beach, Max noticed that Roland had inscribed the vessel's name on the prow with fresh paint, probably that very morning: *Orpheus II*.

"Since when did you have a boat?" Alicia asked, pointing at the ramshackle tub into which Roland had already loaded the diving gear and a couple of baskets with mystifying contents.

"Since three hours ago. One of the local fishermen was about to break her up for firewood, but I convinced him to give her to me in exchange for a favor."

"A favor?" asked Max. "I think you're the one who's done him a favor."

"You're welcome to remain onshore if you'd prefer to have first-class accommodation, sire," retorted Roland. "Come on, all aboard."

Max decided to keep his mouth shut and not wrestle with Roland's pride. As far as he was concerned, the expression *aboard* seemed inappropriate for the vessel in question. However, once they'd covered the first fifteen meters and he could see they were still afloat, Max thought better of it and opted not to judge the boat by its hopeless appearance.

"Well, what do you think, my lord?" joked Roland.

"Fit for a prince, cabin boy."

In fact, the boat moved swiftly in response to Roland's energetic rowing and clearly had a lot more life in it than Max had originally imagined.

"I've brought along a small contraption that may surprise you," said Roland.

Max looked at one of the covered baskets and lifted the lid a centimeter or two.

"What's in here?" he murmured.

"An underwater window," Roland explained. "Really it's just a box with some glass at one end. If you place it on the surface of the water, you can see to the bottom without diving in. That's why it's like a window."

Max pointed at his sister Alicia.

"This way, at least you'll be able to see something, too," he said, teasing her.

"Who says I'm going to stay here? I'm the one who's going down today," she replied.

"You? You don't even know how to dive!" cried Max, trying to wind his sister up.

"If you call what you did the other day diving, no, I don't," responded Alicia, not wanting to start a war.

Roland continued rowing, staying well out of their argument. Finally he stopped the boat some thirty meters from the shore. Beneath them, stretched out on the bottom of the sea, the dark shadow of the *Orpheus* waited like some gigantic shark lurking on the sand. Roland opened one of the baskets and pulled out a rusty anchor attached to a thick, frayed rope. When Max saw the state of the equipment, he assumed that all these bits and pieces were part of what Roland had bargained for in order to save the miserable rowing boat from a dignified and fitting end.

"Careful, it'll splash!" cried Roland as he threw the anchor into the sea. It plummeted in a vertical line, raising a small cloud of bubbles and taking most of the rope with it.

Roland let the current drag the boat along a few meters, then fastened the end of the anchor's rope to a ring that hung from the prow. The boat swayed gently in the waves and the rope tensed, making the wooden structure creak. Max threw a suspicious look at the joints of the hull.

"She's not going to sink, Max. Trust me," Roland said, taking the underwater window out of its basket and placing it on the surface.

"That's what they said on the *Titanic*," Max replied.

Alicia leaned over to look through the box and for the first time saw the hull of the *Orpheus* lying on the bottom of the sea.

"It's incredible!" she gasped.

Roland smiled happily and handed her a mask and a pair of flippers.

"Wait till you see her close up," he said as he put on his gear.

The first to jump into the water was Alicia. Roland, sitting on the edge of the boat, gave Max a reassuring look.

"Don't worry. I'll keep an eye on her. She'll be all right," he said.

Roland jumped into the sea and joined Alicia, who was waiting for him about three meters beyond the boat. They both waved at Max and, a few seconds later, disappeared beneath the surface.

◆ ◆ ◆

Under the water, Roland took Alicia's hand and guided her above the wreck of the *Orpheus*. The temperature was lower than the last time he'd dived there, and he knew that the farther down they went, the colder it would be. Roland was used to this phenomenon. It happened sometimes during the first days of summer, especially when cold currents from the open sea flowed strongly below a depth of six or seven meters. In view of this, Roland decided that he wouldn't allow Alicia or Max to dive down with him to the hull of the *Orpheus* that day. There would be plenty more days in the summer when they could attempt it.

Alicia and Roland swam along the length of the sunken ship, which lay in the spectral light of the seabed. Every now and then they stopped to come up for air and have another look at her from the surface.

Roland sensed Alicia's excitement and didn't take his eyes off her. He knew that if he wanted to enjoy a peaceful dive, it would have to be on his own. When he went diving with someone, especially with beginners, he couldn't help behaving like an underwater nanny. Still, he was particularly pleased to share with his friends the magical world that for years had seemed to belong only to him. He felt like a guide in some bewitching attraction, leading visitors on an incredible journey above a submerged cathedral.

The watery scenery offered other incentives, too. He liked to look at Alicia's body moving under the surface. With each stroke, he could see the muscles on her torso and legs tense beneath her pale skin. In fact, he felt more comfortable watching her like this, when she wasn't aware of his gaze. The next time they came up to the surface for air, the rowboat was at least ten meters away. Alicia smiled excitedly. Roland returned her smile, but deep down he felt that the best thing to do would be to return to the boat.

"Can we go down to the ship and go inside?" Alicia asked, gasping as she spoke.

Roland noticed that her arms were covered in goose pimples.

"Not today," he replied. "Let's go back to the boat."

Alicia saw a flicker of anxiety cross Roland's face.

"Is anything the matter?"

Roland smiled calmly and shook his head. He didn't want to talk about five-degree underwater currents just then. But suddenly, as he watched Alicia swim off toward the boat, his heart skipped a beat. A dark shadow was moving beneath his feet along the bottom of the bay. Alicia turned to look at him. Roland signaled to her to go on and then put his head in the water to inspect the ocean bed.

A black shape—it looked like a large fish—was gliding with sinuous movements around the hull of the *Orpheus*. For a moment Roland thought it might be a shark, but after a second glance, he realized he was wrong. He swam after Alicia, constantly looking back at the strange creature that seemed to be following them.

The silhouette twisted and turned in the shadow of the *Orpheus*, itself avoiding direct exposure to the light. Now Roland could make out a long body, rather like the body of a large snake, enveloped in flashes of deadly luminosity. Roland looked up toward the boat. It was still some distance away. The shadow underneath him seemed to change direction, and Roland saw that it had come into the light and was rising toward them.

Praying that Alicia had not seen it, he grabbed the girl by her arm and started swimming as fast as he could toward the rowboat. Startled, she gave him a puzzled look.

"Swim to the boat! Quickly!" shouted Roland.

Alicia couldn't understand what was happening, but there was such panic on Roland's face that she didn't stop to argue. Roland's shout alerted Max, who watched his friend and Alicia swimming desperately toward him. A moment later Max noticed the dark shadow rising beneath the water.

"Dear God!" he whispered.

In the water, Roland pushed Alicia toward the hull of the rowboat. Max rushed to grab hold of his sister and started trying to pull her out. Alicia kicked her flippers as hard as she could, and with one last pull from Max she managed to fall into the boat on top of her brother. Roland took a deep breath and prepared to do the same.

As Max offered him a hand, Roland could see the terror on his friend's face at what was emerging behind him. He felt his hand slipping from Max's grip. Something told him he wouldn't get out of the water alive. A cold embrace wrapped itself around his legs and, with unimaginable strength, dragged him down toward the depths.

◆ ◆ ◆

After the first few moments of sheer panic, Roland opened his eyes and saw what was dragging him down to the ocean bed. For an instant he thought he was hallucinating, for what Roland saw was not a solid form but what seemed to be some highly concentrated liquid, a feverish moving sculpture that was constantly changing as he tried to free himself from its mortal embrace.

The water creature twisted around and Roland was confronted with the ghostly face he had seen in his dreams, the face of the clown. The clown opened up two enormous jaws filled with long, jagged teeth as sharp as butcher's knives, and its eyes grew in size until they were as big as saucers. Roland was running out of air. The creature, whatever it was, could change into whatever it wanted, and its intentions seemed clear: It wanted to drag Roland inside the sunken ship. As Roland wondered how long he'd be able to hold his breath before giving up and breathing in water, he realized that the light around him had disappeared. He was inside the bowels of the *Orpheus*, surrounded by total darkness.

♦ ♦ ♦

Max swallowed hard as he put on his mask and prepared to jump into the water in search of his friend. He was aware that a rescue attempt was absurd. For a start, he barely knew how to dive and even supposing he did, he couldn't begin to imagine what would happen if, once he was underwater, that strange thing that had trapped Roland came after him. And yet he couldn't just sit in the boat and let his friend die. As he was putting on his flippers, he thought of a thousand reasonable explanations for what had just happened. Roland had suffered a cramp, or he'd had some sort of fit because of a change in the water temperature...any theory was better than having to accept that what he'd seen dragging Roland to the depths was real.

Before jumping in, he exchanged one last glance with Alicia. His sister was clearly caught between her wish to save Roland and panic at the thought that her brother might share the same fate. Before common sense could dissuade them both, Max jumped into the waters of the bay above the hull of the *Orpheus*. He kicked his flippers and swam in the direction of the ship's prow, the place where he'd last seen Roland before he vanished. Through the cracks in the hull below, Max thought he could see flashing lights moving toward a space that gave off a faint glow: It was the breach opened by the rocks in the bilge twenty-five years before. He swam toward it. It looked as if someone had lit hundreds of candles inside the wreck.

When he was situated vertically above the entrance to the vessel, he rose to the surface to take in more air, then dived down until he reached the hull. Descending over ten meters turned out to be much more difficult than he'd imagined. Halfway down he began to feel a painful pressure in his ears, and he thought his eardrums were going to explode. When he reached the cold current, all the muscles in his body tensed like steel cables, and he had to kick his flippers with all his might so that the current didn't drag him away like a leaf in the wind. Max held on firmly to the edge of the hull and struggled to compose himself. His lungs were on fire and he knew he was only one step away from panicking. He looked up at the surface and saw the rowboat's tiny form; it seemed to be miles away. He realized that if he didn't act immediately, diving all the way down would have served no purpose.

The glow seemed to be coming from inside the hold. As Max swam toward it the ghostly landscape of the sunken ship came into view. It looked like a macabre underwater catacomb. He entered a corridor in which shreds of tattered canvas floated by like jellyfish. At the end of the corridor was a half-open hatch, which seemed to be the source of the light. Ignoring the repulsive caresses of the rotten canvas on his skin, he grabbed hold of the handle and pulled as hard as he could.

The hatch led to one of the main compartments in the hold. In the middle of it, Roland was struggling to escape from the water creature that had now adopted the shape of the clown. The light Max had seen blazed from its eyes, cruel and disproportionately large for its face. As Max burst into the hold, the creature raised its head and looked at him. Max felt an instinctive urge to flee, but the sight of his trapped friend forced him to remain, confronting the wild and angry eyes. The creature's face changed and Max recognized the stone angel from the cemetery.

Roland's body stopped writhing and went limp, and the creature let go of him. Without waiting for a reaction, Max swam over to his friend and grabbed him by the arm. Roland was unconscious. If Max didn't take him up to the surface in the next few seconds, he would die. Max pulled him toward the hatch but at that moment, the creature with the face of an angel and the body of a clown threw itself on Max, displaying two sharp claws and a row of fangs. Max pushed his fist through the creature's face. It was only water, but it was so cold that mere contact with it produced a searing pain. Once more, Dr. Cain was showing off his box of tricks.

Max pulled his arm away. The apparition vanished and, with it, the light. Using what little air he had left, Max dragged Roland down the corridor in the hold toward the outside of the hull. His lungs felt as if they were about to burst, and unable to hold his breath another second, he exhaled all the air he had kept in. Then, grabbing hold of Roland's unconscious body, he flapped his way toward the surface, thinking he would lose consciousness himself at any moment.

The agony of those last few meters seemed endless. When at last he reached the surface, he felt as if he'd been reborn. Alicia threw herself into the water and swam toward them. Max took a few deep breaths, fighting against the sharp pain in his chest. It wasn't easy to get Roland into the rowboat, and Max noticed that as Alicia struggled to lift the dead weight of his body, she scratched her arms on the splintered wood.

Once they had managed to haul him into the boat, they placed him on his side and pressed on his back repeatedly, forcing his lungs to expel the water he had inhaled. Her arms bleeding, Alicia seized Roland and tried to force him to breathe. Finally, she took a deep breath, and, pinching the boy's nostrils, she blew frantically into Roland's mouth. She had to do this five times before Roland's body reacted with a violent jerk, and he began to spit out seawater and go into spasms.

At last Roland opened his eyes and his skin began, very slowly, to regain its usual color. Max helped him to sit up and gradually he began to breathe normally.

"I'm all right," Roland stammered, raising a hand to try to reassure his friends.

Alicia burst into tears, sobbing as Max had never seen her do before. He waited a couple of minutes until Roland was able to sit up on his own, then took the oars and started rowing toward the shore. Roland looked at him without saying a word. Max had saved his life. He knew that the look in Roland's eyes, full of despair and gratitude, would remain with him forever.

♦ ♦ ♦

They placed Roland on his bed in the beach hut and covered him with blankets. None of them felt like talking about what had happened, at least not for the moment. It was the first time the threat posed by the Prince of Mist had become so painfully real, and it was difficult to find words with which to express the terror and anxiety they were all feeling. Common sense seemed to dictate that the best thing to do was attend to their immediate needs, and that was what they did. Roland kept a basic first aid kit in the hut, and Max used it to clean Alicia's wounds. Roland fell asleep a few minutes later. Alicia watched over him, her face distraught.

"He's going to be all right. He's exhausted, that's all," said Max.

"What about you? You saved his life," said Alicia, her voice unable to hide her concern. "No one could have done what you did, Max."

"He would have done the same thing for me," said Max, who wasn't ready to talk about it.

"How are you feeling?"

"The truth?" Max asked.

Alicia nodded.

"I think I'm going to throw up," Max said, smiling faintly. "I haven't felt this bad in all my life."

Alicia hugged him tightly. Max stood still, his arms hanging by his sides, not knowing whether this was an outpouring of sisterly love or a reaction to the terror she had experienced earlier when they were trying to revive Roland.

"I love you, Max," Alicia whispered in his ear. "Do you hear me?"

Max didn't reply. He was perplexed. Alicia released him from her embrace and turned toward the door of the hut, with her back to him. Max noticed that she was crying.

"Don't ever forget it, little brother," she whispered. "Now get some sleep. I'll do the same."

"If I fall asleep now, I'll never get up again," Max sighed.

Five minutes later, the friends were sound asleep in the beach hut, and nothing in the whole world could have awoken them.

14

THE SUN WAS SETTING when Victor Kray stopped about a hundred meters from the beach house where the Carvers had taken up residence. This was the same house where the only woman he had ever loved, Eva Gray, had given birth to Jacob Fleischmann. To see the white facade again opened old wounds, just when he had hoped they had healed forever. All the lights were out and the place looked deserted. Victor Kray assumed that the youngsters must still be in the town with Roland.

The lighthouse keeper walked straight on through the white fence that surrounded the beach house. The same door and the same windows he remembered shone in the last rays of sun. He crossed the garden toward the backyard, and from there he walked out into the field behind the house. The forest rose in the distance, and close to the forest's edge stood the walled garden. He had not been back there for a long time, and he stopped to observe it from afar, dreading what was hidden behind its walls. Through the dark bars of the gate, a thick mist was spreading toward him.

Victor Kray had never felt so old, or so frightened. The fear that gnawed at his soul was the same fear he'd experienced decades ago in the narrow alleys of that industrial suburb, where he had heard the voice of the Prince of Mist for the first time. Now, in the twilight of his life, that circle seemed to be closing and, with each new twist of the game, the old man sensed that there were no longer any aces up his sleeve.

The lighthouse keeper now advanced steadily toward the enclosure and soon the mist reached up to his waist. He thrust a trembling hand into his pocket and pulled out his old revolver, carefully loaded before he left the cottage, and a powerful flashlight. Weapon in hand, he entered the walled garden, then turned on the flashlight. Its beam revealed an extraordinary scene. Victor Kray lowered the gun and rubbed his eyes, thinking he must be imagining things. Something had gone wrong—at least, this wasn't what he'd expected to find. He sliced the beam through the mist once more. It wasn't an illusion: The garden of statues was empty.

Disconcerted, he drew closer to examine the vacant pedestals. While he tried to put his thoughts in some sort of order, he heard the faraway rumble of a new storm approaching and lifted his head to scan the horizon. A blanket of dark, murky clouds spilled over the sea like an inky stain. A flash of lightning split the skies and the echo of thunder rumbled toward the coast, a drumroll announcing the onset of battle. Victor Kray listened to the insistent growl of the storm that was gathering at sea, and, remembering that he had gazed at that same vision on board the *Orpheus* twenty-five years before, he finally understood what was about to happen.

◆ ◆ ◆

Max woke up drenched in a cold sweat and it took him a few moments to realize where he was. He could feel his heart pounding. A few feet away he recognized a familiar face: Alicia, asleep next to Roland; then he remembered that he was in the beach hut. He could have sworn he'd slept only for an instant, although in fact he'd been asleep for almost an hour. He got up quietly and went outside for some fresh air. Harrowing images of a nightmare in which he and Roland were trapped inside the *Orpheus* began to recede from his mind.

The beach was deserted and the high tide had carried Roland's rowboat out to sea. Soon the currents would drag the small vessel even farther away, and it would be forever lost in the immensity of the ocean. Max walked down to the shore and dampened his face and shoulders with cool water. Then he went over to a small cove and sat on the rocks, dipping his feet in the water, hoping to recover the calm that sleep had not provided him.

Max knew there had to be some hidden logic behind the events of the last few days. He could sense everything was part of a complex mechanism that was slowly but surely coming together, and at its center was the tragedy of Jacob Fleischmann. It was all connected—everything, from the mysterious visits to the walled garden he'd seen in the old films to the indescribable creature that had almost taken their lives that very afternoon.

Bearing in mind what had happened that day, Max realized they couldn't allow themselves the luxury of waiting for the next meeting with Dr. Cain: They had to anticipate his movements and try to foresee what his next step would be. For Max there was only one way of finding out, and that was to follow the trail Jacob Fleischmann had left years ago in his films.

Without bothering to wake Alicia and Roland, Max got on his bike and rode off toward the beach house. In the distance, above the line of the horizon, a dark point appeared from nowhere and began to expand like a cloud of lethal gas.

♦ ♦ ♦

Back at home, Max threaded a film onto the reel of the projector. The temperature had plummeted while he was cycling over, and now it was getting even colder. The first echoes of the storm could be heard between the occasional gusts of wind that banged against the shutters. Before watching the film, Max hurried upstairs and threw on some warm clothes. The old wooden structure of the house, assailed by the wind, creaked beneath his feet. While he was changing his clothes, Max looked out of his bedroom window and saw the approaching storm covering the sky with a cloak of darkness, bringing the onslaught of night a couple of hours early. He secured the window lock and went downstairs to turn on the projector.

Once more, the images projected on the wall stirred into life. This time the camera showed a familiar scene: the corridors of the house by the beach. Max recognized the inside of the very room he was sitting in. The decor and the furniture were different, and the house looked quite opulent as the camera panned out, displaying the walls and windows. It was as if a trapdoor had been opened into the past, allowing Max to visit the house more than ten years before.

After a couple of minutes on the ground floor, the camera led the spectator upstairs. On reaching the landing, the camera traveled along the hallway until it came to the door at the end — the door to the bedroom occupied by Irina until her accident. The door opened and the camera entered, scanning the dark, empty room before stopping in front of the wardrobe.

A few seconds went by and nothing happened; the camera didn't register any movement in the room. Suddenly, the door of the wardrobe sprang open and hit the wall, swinging on its hinges. Max tried to make out what was inside. A hand in a white glove appeared from the shadows holding a shining object that hung from a chain. Max guessed what was coming next: Dr. Cain emerged from the wardrobe and smiled at the camera.

Max felt cold dread clutching his stomach as he recognized the round object the Prince of Mist was holding in his hand. It was the pocket watch his father had given him, the one he'd lost inside Jacob Fleischmann's tomb. Now it was in the hands of the magician, who had somehow taken his most prized possession back into the ghostly dimension of these black-and-white images.

The camera closed in on the watch and Max could clearly see that the hands were turning backward at an incredible speed, going faster and faster until he could no longer focus on them. After a while, the watch began to give off smoke and sparks until at last it caught fire.

Max watched the scene, spellbound, unable to take his eyes off the burning watch. A moment later, the camera jumped to the bedroom wall, zooming in on an old dressing table with a mirror. The camera drew closer to the mirror and then stopped, revealing the identity of the person who was holding it.

Max gulped; he was finally face-to-face with the person who had made these films years ago in this very house. He recognized the childish grin of the boy who was filming himself. He was a few years younger, but the features and the eyes were the same as the ones he had gotten to know in the course of the last few days. It was Roland.

The film got stuck inside the projector, and the still that was caught in front of the lens slowly began to melt on the screen. Max turned off the machine and clenched his fists to stop them from shaking. Jacob Fleischmann and Roland were one and the same person.

A flash of lightning invaded the darkened room, and Max suddenly noticed a figure on the other side of the window, rapping on the windowpanes. Max turned on the light in the living room and recognized the pale face of Victor Kray. From his terrified expression, it looked as though he'd just witnessed an apparition. Max went over to the door and let the old man in. They had a lot to talk about.

15

Max handed the old lighthouse keeper a cup of hot tea and waited for him to warm up.

Victor Kray was shaking, and Max didn't know whether this was because of the cold wind raised by the storm or the fear the old man clearly could not hide.

"What were you doing out there, Mr. Kray?" asked Max.

"I've been to the walled garden," the old man answered, trying to compose himself.

Victor Kray sipped some tea, then placed his cup on the table.

"Where's Roland, Max?" he asked nervously.

"Why do you want to know?" In view of his latest discovery, Max didn't even bother to conceal his suspicion.

The lighthouse keeper seemed to sense Max's distrust and began to gesture with his hands, as if he wanted to explain but couldn't find the words.

"Max, something terrible is going to happen tonight if we don't stop it," Victor Kray said at last, aware that his words sounded far from convincing. "I need to know where Roland is. His life is in great danger."

Max examined the old man's face carefully. He felt he couldn't believe a word the lighthouse keeper said.

"Which life is that, Mr. Kray, Roland's or Jacob Fleischmann's?"

The old man gave a weary sigh.

"I don't think I understand you, Max," he murmured.

"I think you do. I know you lied to me, Mr. Kray," Max said accusingly. "And I know who Roland really is. You've been lying to us all along. What I want to know is why?"

Victor Kray stood up and walked over to one of the windows, glancing outside as if he were expecting a visit. A rumble of thunder shook the house. The storm was drawing closer by the minute, and Max could hear the sound of huge breakers crashing against the beach.

"Tell me where Roland is, Max," the old man insisted,

his eyes still glued to the window. "There's no time to lose."

"I'm not sure I can trust you. If you want me to help you, you'll have to tell me the truth," Max demanded. He wasn't going to let Victor Kray keep him in the dark again.

The old man turned and looked at him severely, but Max held his gaze to show that he was not intimidated. The lighthouse keeper seemed to understand the situation and collapsed into an armchair, defeated.

"All right, Max. I'll tell you the truth, if that's what you want."

Max sat in front of him and nodded, ready to listen.

"Almost everything I told you the other day in the lighthouse is true," the old man began. "My friend Fleischmann had promised Dr. Cain that he would give him his first-born son in exchange for Eva Gray's love. A year after the wedding, when I'd already lost touch with both of them, Fleischmann began to receive visits from Dr. Cain, who reminded him of their pact. Fleischmann tried everything to avoid having a child, to the point of destroying his own marriage. After the wreck of the *Orpheus*, I felt it was my duty to write to them and tell them they were free of the sentence that had made them unhappy for so many years. I thought that the threat posed by Dr. Cain had been buried forever beneath the sea. Or I was stupid enough to convince myself of that. Fleischmann felt guilty that he was in debt to me, and he wanted all three of us — Eva, himself, and me — to be together again, as we had been during our years at university. That was absurd, of course. Too much had happened. Even so, Fleischmann went ahead with his plans to build the house by the beach, and soon afterward their son Jacob was born. The little boy was a blessing from heaven and made them happy to be alive once more. Or at least that's how it seemed, but from the night of his birth I knew that something wasn't right because that night, in the early hours before dawn, I dreamed once more about Dr. Cain.

"As the boy grew, Fleischmann and Eva were so blinded by their happiness they couldn't perceive the threat that still hung over them. They were both completely devoted to the boy and they gave in to him too easily. Never was a child so indulged as Jacob Fleischmann. But, little by little, the signs of Cain's presence became more evident. One day, when Jacob was five years old, he got lost while playing behind the house. Fleischmann and Eva desperately looked for him for hours, but there was no sign of the boy. When night fell, Fleischmann took a flashlight and went into the forest, fearing that the child might have gotten lost among the undergrowth or had an accident. Then he remembered that when they were building the house, six years earlier, there had been a small, empty enclosure near the entrance to the forest. Apparently, it had once been a kind of pound, a place where animals were kept before they were put down, until it was demolished at the turn of the century. That night, a gut feeling told Fleischmann that perhaps the boy had ventured inside the enclosure and become trapped. He was partly correct, but his son wasn't the only thing he discovered.

"The walled enclosure, which had been deserted, was now peopled with statues. Jacob was playing among the figures when his father found him and led him away. A couple of days later, Fleischmann paid me a visit in the lighthouse and told me what had happened. He made me swear that if anything should happen to him, I would take care of his child. That was just the beginning. Fleischmann didn't tell his wife about the mysterious incidents that were occurring around his son, but in his heart he knew there would be no escape and that sooner or later Cain would return to claim what belonged to him."

"What happened the night Jacob drowned?" Max interrupted, guessing at the reply but hoping that the old man's words might prove him wrong.

Victor Kray lowered his head before replying.

"On a day like today, the twenty-third of June, the same date the *Orpheus* was shipwrecked, there was a violent storm out at sea. The fishermen hurried to secure their boats and the townspeople closed all their doors and windows, just as they'd done the night of the shipwreck a few years before. The place became a ghost town. I was in the lighthouse and a terrible fear took hold of me, an intuition: The boy was in danger. I crossed the deserted streets and hurried here as fast as I could. Jacob had stepped out of the house and was walking along the beach, heading for the water's edge, where the waves were breaking with ferocious power. It was raining hard and visibility was poor, but I was able to make out a shining form that had emerged from the water and was stretching out two long arms, like tentacles, toward the child. Jacob seemed to be hypnotized by the water creature and was drawing nearer. It was Cain, I was quite sure of that, but for once it seemed as if all his identities had fused into a single shape that was constantly changing...I can't really describe what I saw...."

"I've seen it myself," Max interrupted, saving the old man a description of the creature he had set eyes on only a few hours before. "Go on."

"I wondered why Fleischmann and his wife weren't there trying to save the boy, so I looked over at the house. A troupe of circus figures whose bodies seemed to be made of stone was holding them back on the porch.

"The statues from the walled garden," agreed Max.

The old man nodded.

"All I could think of was that I had to save the child. The creature had taken him in its arms and was dragging him into the sea. I hurled myself against its tentacles and fell straight through it. The enormous watery shape faded back into the darkness. Jacob had gone under. I dived a few times until I found his body and was able to rescue him and take him back to the surface. I hauled him onto the sand, far from the water's edge, and tried to revive him. The statues had disappeared along with Cain. Fleischmann and Eva ran toward me to help the boy, but by the time they arrived we couldn't feel his pulse. We took him into the house and tried everything, but it was no use: The boy was dead. Fleischmann was beside himself with grief and he ran outside, shouting at the storm and offering his own life to Cain in exchange for the life of his son. Minutes later, inexplicably, Jacob opened his eyes. He was in shock. He didn't recognize us and couldn't even remember his own name. Eva wrapped the boy in a blanket and took him upstairs, where she put him to bed. When, after a while, she came down again, she walked over to me and calmly told me that if the boy continued to live with them, his life would be in danger. She asked me to take care of him and bring him up as if he were my own son, the son who, if fate had taken a different course, might have been ours. Fleischmann didn't dare enter the house. I accepted what Eva Gray was asking of me and saw in her eyes that she was renouncing the one thing that had given her life any meaning. The following day, I took the boy home with me. I never saw the Fleischmanns again."

There was a long pause. The old man was probably trying to hold back his tears, but his face was hidden behind his pale, wrinkled hands.

"A year later I found out that Fleischmann had passed away from a deadly infection he had caught after being bitten by a wild dog. Even now, I don't know whether Eva Gray is still alive.... We let the townspeople think Jacob had drowned...."

Max searched the old man's face. He looked so distraught that Max realized he'd misjudged him.

"You invented a story about Roland's parents, you even gave him a new name...."

Kray nodded, admitting the greatest secret of his life to a thirteen-year-old boy he'd met only a couple of times.

"So Roland doesn't know who he really is?" asked Max.

The old man shook his head repeatedly, and Max noticed that there were tears of anger in his eyes—eyes that had been damaged by all those years of vigil from the top of the lighthouse.

"Then who is buried in Jacob Fleischmann's plot in the cemetery?" Max asked.

"Nobody," replied the old man. "Officially, no one ever built that tomb and there was no funeral. The mausoleum you saw the other day simply appeared in the local cemetery the week after the storm. The people in the town thought that Fleischmann had it built for his son."

"I don't understand," Max replied, "If it wasn't Fleischmann, then who put it there and why?"

Victor Kray smiled bitterly.

"Cain," he replied at last. "Cain put it there. He's been reserving it for Jacob."

"My God," whispered Max, realizing that perhaps he'd wasted precious time, forcing the old man to confess the entire story. "We must get Roland away from the beach hut immediately...."

♦ ♦ ♦

Alicia woke up to the sound of waves crashing on the beach. Night had fallen and the rain was pounding down on the roof of the hut as if the storm was trying to destroy it. She sat up in a daze and saw that Roland was still lying on the bed, whispering incoherently in his sleep. Max wasn't there. She walked over to the door, opened it, and took a quick look at the beach.

A ghostly mist was creeping up from the sea toward

the hut, and Alicia could hear dozens of voices whispering from its midst. She slammed the door and leaned against it, determined not to let panic take over. Startled by the banging of the door, Roland opened his eyes and pulled himself up, not quite understanding how he'd gotten there.

"What's happening?"

Alicia opened her mouth to speak, but something stopped her. Roland watched in amazement as the thick mist filtered through every joint in the hut and entwined itself around her. The girl screamed and the door on which she'd been leaning flew outside, torn off its hinges by an invisible force. Roland jumped out of bed and ran over to help Alicia, who was being pulled away toward the sea, wrapped in a tentacle of eerie mist. A figure stood in his way. Roland recognized the watery specter that had pulled him down to the ocean depths. The clown's wolfish face lit up.

"Hello, Jacob," the voice whispered behind gelatinous lips. "Now we're going to have some fun."

Roland punched the liquid form and it disintegrated in the air, water cascading down onto the floor. As he rushed outside, Roland was struck by the force of the storm. A swirling dome of dense, purple clouds had formed above the bay from which a blinding flash of lightning shot out toward one of the peaks of the cliff, exploding

tons of rocks, which rained down in a shower of frag-
ments over the beach.

Alicia screamed, struggling to free herself from the
lethal embrace that imprisoned her, and Roland ran
across the stones toward her. He tried to reach out and
grab her hand but a large wave knocked him over. When
he got up, the whole bay was shaking beneath his feet,
and Roland heard an enormous roar that seemed to be
rising from the depths of the sea. The boy took a few
steps back, struggling to keep his balance, and saw a
gigantic luminous form emerging from the waters, sending waves that were several meters high in all directions.
In the center of the bay, the shape of a mast was beginning to appear. Slowly, before Roland's incredulous eyes,
the *Orpheus* was floating to the surface, enveloped in a
supernatural aura.

Standing on the bridge, wrapped in his cloak, Cain
pointed a silver wand to the heavens, and a new bolt of
lightning flashed above him, illuminating the *Orpheus*.
The magician's cruel laughter echoed through the bay,
while the spectral tentacle dropped Alicia at his feet.

"You're the one I want, Jacob," Cain's voice whispered in Roland's mind. "If you don't want her to die,
come and get her...."

16

Max was cycling through the rain when a bright flash of lightning startled him. It revealed the sight of the *Orpheus* re-emerging from the depths, glowing with a hypnotic light that emanated from her metal frame. Cain's old ship was once more sailing across the furious waters of the bay. Max pedaled on desperately, afraid that he wouldn't reach the beach hut in time. He'd left the lighthouse keeper behind—the old man couldn't possibly keep up with him. When Max reached the edge of the beach, he jumped off his bike and sprinted toward Roland's hut. He discovered that the door had been torn clean off its hinges. On the shore, he caught sight of the paralyzed outline of his friend, standing spellbound as he watched the ghostly ship plough through the waves. Max thanked the heavens and ran over to embrace him.

"Are you all right?" he shouted against the howl of wind.

Roland looked back at him, startled, like a wounded animal unable to escape its predator. Max saw in him the childish face that had held the camera in front of the mirror, and he shuddered.

"He's got Alicia," said Roland at last.

Max knew his friend couldn't really understand what was going on, but he felt that trying to explain it would only complicate things.

"Whatever happens," Max shouted, "you have to get away from him. Do you hear me? You must get away from Cain!"

Ignoring his words, Roland waded into the sea until the swell reached his waist. Max went after him and tried to bring him back, but Roland, who was stronger, shoved him aside and forged on into the water.

"Wait!" shouted Max. "You don't know what's happening! You're the one he's looking for!"

"I know," Roland replied.

Max watched his friend dive into the waves and surface a couple of meters farther on, swimming toward the *Orpheus*. The wiser half of his soul begged him loud and clear to run back to the hut and hide under the bed until everything was over. As usual, Max listened to the other side and threw himself into the waves, quite sure that this time he wouldn't make it back alive.

◆ ◆ ◆

Cain's long, gloved fingers closed like pincers around Alicia's wrist. The magician pulled her along the slippery deck of the *Orpheus*, while she struggled frantically to free herself. Cain turned around and, lifting her effortlessly into the air, put his face so close to hers that the girl could see his eyes burning with anger. They changed color from blue to gold, and his pupils dilated.

"I'm not going to say this twice," the magician's voice was lifeless, as cold as steel. "Keep still or you'll be sorry. Understood?"

The magician increased the pressure of his fingers. Alicia was afraid that if he didn't stop he'd pulverize the bones in her wrist as if they were brittle clay. Realizing that it was useless to oppose him, she nodded nervously. Cain loosened his grip and smiled. There was no pity or courtesy in that smile, only hatred. He let go of her and Alicia fell onto the deck, hitting her forehead on the metal. She touched her skin and felt the sharp stinging sensation of an open wound. Without giving her a moment to recover, Cain grabbed her arm again and dragged her toward the bowels of the ship.

"Go on," the magician ordered, pushing her along a corridor that led from the bridge to the cabins.

The walls were black and covered in rust and a slimy coat of seaweed. Inside, the *Orpheus* was swimming in muddy water that gave off a noxious smell and was filled with bits and pieces of debris that swayed with the rocking of the ship on the heavy swell. Cain grabbed Alicia by the hair and opened the door of one of the cabins. A cloud of gas and the stench of stagnant water that had been imprisoned there for twenty-five years filled the air. Alicia held her breath. Still clutching her hair, the magician heaved her toward the door.

"The best suite awaits you, my dear. The captain's cabin for my guest of honor. Enjoy the company."

Cain pushed her inside and shut the heavy door. Alicia fell to her knees and felt around behind her, searching for something to cling to. It was almost pitch-dark in the cabin: The only light came from a narrow porthole, which years of being submerged in the sea had covered with a thick, semi-transparent crust of seaweed and rotting remains. The constant rolling of the ship propelled Alicia against the cabin walls, and she grabbed on to a rusty water pipe. It took her eyes a while to adjust to the dim light, and as she struggled not to think about the penetrating odor that filled the place, she examined the cell Cain had reserved for her. There was no other exit save the door the magician had locked when he left. Alicia looked desperately for a metal bar or some other blunt object with which she could try to force the door open, but she couldn't find anything. As she groped around, her hands touched something that had been leaning against the wall. Alicia took a step back, startled. The barely recognizable remains of the captain of the *Orpheus* fell at her feet, and Alicia suddenly understood who Cain had been referring to when he spoke of her "company." Fate hadn't dealt the Flying Dutchman a good hand. The roar of the stormy sea drowned out her screams.

♦ ♦ ♦

For every meter Roland gained in his approach to the *Orpheus*, the fury of the sea sucked him underwater and returned him to the surface on the crest of a wave, engulfing him in an eddy of foam. Before him, the ship was also locked in combat, assailed by the walls of water pummeling her hull.

As he neared the ship, the violence of the sea made it more difficult to control the direction in which he was heading, and Roland feared that a sudden surge might hurl him against the hull of the *Orpheus*, rendering him unconscious. If that were to happen, the waters would swallow him down greedily, and he would never return to the surface. Roland dived through an enormous wave towering over him and emerged in a valley of murky water as the wave rolled off toward the shore.

The *Orpheus* loomed less than a dozen meters away, and when he saw the steel hull, tinted with a fiery light, he knew he would be unable to climb up to the deck. The only way in was through the gash the rocks had torn open in the hull twenty-five years ago, causing the sinking of the ship. The gap was level with the waterline, and it appeared and disappeared with every new pounding from the waves. Strips of jagged metal surrounded the gaping hole, making it look like the jaws of some enormous beast. The very idea of entering such a death trap terrified Roland, but it was his only chance of reaching Alicia. He struggled through the next wave and, once its crest had passed over him, he hurled himself toward the hole, shooting through it into the darkness like a human torpedo.

◆ ◆ ◆

Victor Kray was gasping for breath as he walked along the path that led through the wild grass down to the bay. The rain and strong wind slowed him down, like invisible hands determined to hold him back. When at last he reached the beach, he saw the *Orpheus* in the middle of the bay swathed in spectral light. She was heading in a straight line toward the cliff. The prow of the ship plunged through the waves, the water sweeping over the deck, raising a cloud of white foam with each new shudder of the ocean. A veil of despair fell over him: His worst fears had come true and he had failed; his mind had been weakened by the passing years and, once again, the Prince of Mist had tricked him. Now all he asked was that it not be too late to save Roland. At that moment, Victor Kray would happily have offered his own life if it could have provided Roland with even the slenderest possibility of escape. And yet he had a dark premonition that perhaps he'd already failed in the promise he had once made to the boy's mother.

Victor Kray walked toward Roland's hut in the vain hope of finding him there. There was no sign of Max or of the girl, and the sight of the front door lying on the beach seemed to confirm his worst fears. Then, suddenly, he felt a glimmer of hope when he realized there was light inside the beach hut. He rushed toward it, calling out Roland's name. The figure of a knife thrower, carved from pale stone yet alive, came out of the shadows to greet him.

"It's a bit late to start having regrets now, Granddad," said the figure, and the old man recognized Cain's voice.

Victor Kray took a step back, but there was someone behind him, and before he was able to react, he felt a dry blow to the back of his neck. Darkness fell.

◆ ◆ ◆

Max saw Roland enter the hull of the *Orpheus* through the breach and realized he was losing strength with each new wave. He could not compare to Roland as a swimmer, and he knew that he'd be unable to stay afloat much longer in the storm unless he could find some way of getting on board the ship. On the other hand, the certainty that great danger awaited them in the bowels of the vessel grew with every passing minute, and Max realized that the magician was drawing them into his lair like bees to honey.

Then came a deafening roar, and Max saw a gigantic wall of water rising behind the stern of the *Orpheus* and approaching the ship at great speed. In a matter of seconds, the impact of the gigantic wave threw the ship against the cliff face, and the prow smashed into the rocks, provoking a violent shockwave along the length of the hull. The mast, with its navigation lights, collapsed over the side of the ship, the head of it plunging into the water only meters away from Max.

Max scrambled toward it, then grabbed hold and

rested a moment to get his breath back. When he looked up, he saw that the fallen mast had provided him with a kind of ladder up to the deck of the ship. Before a new wave could tear it away, Max began to climb, unaware that, leaning on the starboard rail, a motionless figure was waiting for him.

♦ ♦ ♦

As the force of the water swept Roland through the flooded bilge, the boy protected his face with his arms to avoid the blows dealt him by his passage through the shipwreck. He allowed himself to be carried along by the current until a sudden surge flung him against a wall, where he managed to grab hold of a small metal ladder leading to the upper part of the ship.

Roland climbed the narrow steps, then passed through a hatch into the dark vault that housed the ruined engines of the *Orpheus*. He stepped over the broken machinery, reaching the passage that led up to the deck. Once there, he rushed along the corridor lined by cabins until he came to the bridge. It was a strange feeling for Roland, recognizing every corner of the room and all the objects he had seen so often when he went diving. From this vantage point, Roland had a good view over the whole front deck of the *Orpheus*: the waves rushing over it and foaming along the platform of the bridge. Suddenly, Roland felt a tremendous force propelling the *Orpheus* forward, and he watched in astonishment as the cliff seemed to rise up from the shadows just beyond the ship's prow. They were going to hit the rocks.

Roland hurriedly grabbed hold of the helm, but his feet slipped on the film of seaweed covering the floor. He stumbled and collided with an old radio, then his whole body felt the tremendous shock as the hull crashed against the cliff face. Once the worst was over, he stood up and heard a sound close by, a human voice amid the roar of the storm. The sound came again and Roland recognized it: It was Alicia screaming for help somewhere in the ship.

◆ ◆ ◆

The ten meters Max had to climb up the mast to the deck of the *Orpheus* felt more like a hundred. The wood was practically rotted away and was so splintered that, when he finally touched the gunwale, his arms and legs were covered in small stinging cuts. He decided it was better not to stop to examine his wounds and stretched out a hand to grasp the metal rail.

Once he'd gotten a good grip, he launched himself over it and fell onto the deck. A dark shadow passed before him and Max looked up, hoping to see Roland. It was Cain. The magician opened his cloak to show Max a silver object hanging on the end of a chain. The boy recognized the watch he'd lost in Jacob Fleischmann's tomb.

"Were you looking for this?" asked Cain, kneeling next to the boy and dangling the watch in front of him.

"Where's Jacob?" Max demanded, ignoring the mocking expression on Cain's waxen face, which resembled a mask.

"That's the question of the day," replied the magician, "and you're going to help me answer it."

Cain closed his hand around the watch, and Max heard the crunch of metal. When the magician opened his palm again, all that remained of his father's present was an unrecognizable tangle of squashed cogs and screws.

"Time, dear Max, doesn't exist; it's an illusion. Even your friend Copernicus would have guessed the truth if he'd had precisely that—time. Ironic, isn't it?"

Max was busy calculating whether or not it was possible to jump overboard and escape from the magician, but Cain's white glove closed around his neck before he could take another breath.

"What are you going to do with me?" Max groaned.

"What would you do with yourself if you were in my place?"

Max felt Cain's lethal grip cut off his breathing and the blood to his head.

"It's a good question, isn't it?"

The magician let go of Max, dropping him onto the deck. The impact of the rusty metal clouded Max's vision momentarily, and he was overwhelmed by a sudden nausea.

"Why are you pursuing Jacob?" Max stammered, trying to gain time for Roland.

"Business is business, Max. I carried out my part of the deal."

"But what can the life of one child mean to you?" Max pleaded. "You've already had your revenge by killing Dr. Fleischmann, haven't you?"

Cain's face lit up, as if Max had just asked him the very question he'd been waiting to hear since the start of their conversation.

"When a debt is not settled, it gathers interest. But that does not cancel the original debt. That is my rule," hissed the magician. "And it's what I feed on—Jacob's life and the lives of others like him. Do you know how many years I've been roaming around the world, Max? Do you know how many names I've had?"

Max shook his head, giving thanks for every second the magician lost by talking to him.

"Tell me," he replied in a tiny voice, feigning admiration.

Cain smiled triumphantly. At that moment the thing Max had feared happened. Through the noise of the storm came the sound of Roland's voice, calling Alicia's name. Max and the magician looked at one another; they had both heard it. The smile left Cain's face and was immediately replaced by the expression of a bloodthirsty predator.

"Very clever," he whispered.

Max gulped, preparing for the worst.

The magician opened a hand in front of him and Max watched in horror as each of his fingers melted into a long needle. Only a few meters away, Roland shouted again. While Cain turned to look behind him, Max made a dash for the side of the ship, but the magician's claw seized Max by the scruff of his neck, turning him slowly until he was standing face to face with the Prince of Mist.

"A shame your friend isn't half as clever as you are. Perhaps I should make the deal with you. Oh, well... some other time," the magician spat. "See you later, Max. I hope you've learned to dive since our last encounter."

With extreme force, the magician flung Max into the air and back into the sea. The boy's body sailed over ten meters through the sky, then landed among the waves, sinking into the freezing cold water. Max struggled to rise to the surface, thrashing his arms and legs, trying to escape from the deadly current that seemed to be dragging him down into the darkness. Feeling as if his lungs were about to burst, he swam blindly until finally he surfaced a few meters from the rocks. He took in some air and, in an effort to stay afloat, let the waves carry him toward the edge of the rocky wall, where he managed to cling onto a ledge, then clamber up to safety. The sharp stones bit into his skin, and Max was aware of them scraping his arms and legs, but he was so numb with cold he could barely feel the pain. Trying not to faint, he climbed up until he reached a recess among the rocks where the waves couldn't reach him. Only then was he able to rest on the hard stone, still so frightened he couldn't allow himself to believe he'd saved his own life.

17

THE CABIN DOOR OPENED SLOWLY. Alicia, curled up in a dark corner, held her breath and didn't move. The Prince of Mist was outlined in the doorway and his eyes, flashing like hot coals, changed from gold to a deep crimson. Cain entered the cabin and strode over to her. Trying hard to hide the trembling that had seized hold of her, Alicia faced her visitor defiantly. The magician grinned like a dog at her show of arrogance.

"It must run in the family. You're all born heroes," the magician said softly. "I'm beginning to like you."

"What is it you want?" asked Alicia, filling her shaky voice with all the contempt she could muster.

Cain seemed to consider the question. Alicia noticed that his nails were long and sharp, like the tip of a dagger. Cain pointed at her.

"That depends. What do you suggest?" he asked sweetly, his eyes fixed on her face.

"I have nothing to give you," she replied, stealing a glance at the open door.

Cain wagged a finger, guessing her intentions.

"That would not be a good idea," he stated. "Let's go back to our conversation. Why don't we make a deal? An understanding between adults, if you see what I mean."

"What deal?" Alicia replied, trying to avoid Cain's hypnotic eyes, which seemed to be sucking away her willpower, a parasite feeding on her soul.

"That's what I like, so let's talk business. Tell me, Alicia, would you like to save Jacob — sorry, I mean Roland? He's a good-looking boy," said the magician, savoring every last word of his offer.

"What would you want in exchange? My life?" Alicia replied. The words came out of her mouth before she'd even had time to think.

The magician crossed his arms and frowned, looking pensive. Alicia noticed that he never blinked.

"I was thinking of something else, my dear," Cain explained, stroking his lower lip with the tip of his forefinger. "How about the life of your first born?"

Cain moved toward Alicia and brought his face up close to hers so that she could smell the sweet, nauseating stench of his breath. Looking straight into his eyes, she spit in the magician's face.

"Go to hell," she said, reining in her anger.

The drops of saliva evaporated as if she'd spit onto a burning metal plate.

"My dear girl, that's exactly where I've come from."

Slowly, the magician stretched out his naked hand toward Alicia's face. She closed her eyes and felt the icy touch of his fingers as the long, sharp nails rested on her forehead. The wait seemed endless. At last, Alicia heard his footsteps moving away and the heavy metal door of the cabin closing behind him. An odor of decay seeped through the cracks around the door like steam hissing from a pressure cooker. Alicia felt like weeping, like banging on the walls to satisfy her anger, but she needed to stay in control and keep her mind clear. She had to get out of there and she didn't have much time.

She walked over to the door and felt around the edges in search of a gap or chink that she could use to force it open. Nothing. Cain had entombed her in a rusty sarcophagus in the company of the old captain's bones. At that moment, a huge jolt shook the boat and Alicia fell to the floor. A few seconds later, she heard a dull sound coming from the bowels of the ship. Alicia pressed her ear to the metal and listened carefully; it was the unmistakable rush of running water. A lot of water. Alicia, in a panic, realized what was happening: The hull was being flooded and the *Orpheus* was sinking once more. This time she was unable to suppress a terrified scream.

◆ ◆ ◆

Roland had searched for Alicia all over the ship, but with no success. The *Orpheus* was transformed into a watery catacomb, a labyrinth of interminable corridors and barred doors. The magician could have hidden her in dozens of different places. Roland returned to the bridge and tried to work out where she might be trapped. Then came the crash and the whole vessel shuddered, making Roland lose his balance on the damp, slippery floor. Cain materialized out of the shadows, as if he had emerged through the cracked metal floor.

"We're sinking, Jacob," the magician explained calmly, pointing around him. "Timing has never been your strong point, has it?"

"I don't know what you're talking about. Where's Alicia?" Roland demanded, ready to pounce on his opponent.

The magician closed his eyes and joined the palms of his hands together as if in prayer.

"Somewhere on this ship," he replied. "If you were stupid enough to follow her here, don't ruin it now. Do you want to save her life, Jacob?"

"My name is Roland," the boy snapped.

"Roland, Jacob...what does it matter if it's one name or the other? I have quite a few names myself. What is your wish, Roland? Do you want to save your friend?"

"Where have you hidden her?" Roland replied. "Damn you! Where is she?"

The magician rubbed his hands, as if he were feeling cold.

"Do you know how long a ship like this takes to sink, Jacob? Don't tell me. A couple of minutes at the most. Surprising, isn't it?" laughed Cain.

"You want Jacob, or whatever I'm called," Roland declared. "Well, you've got him; I'm not going to escape. So let her go."

"How original, Jacob," intoned the magician, drawing closer. "Your time's running out, Jacob. One minute."

The *Orpheus* began to list to starboard. The water flooding the boat roared beneath their feet, and the damaged metal structure shivered as the furious sea spread through it like acid dissolving a cardboard toy.

"What do you want me to do?" begged Roland. "What do you want of me?"

"Good, Jacob. I see you're beginning to understand.

I hope you'll carry out the part of the agreement your father was unable to fulfill," the magician replied. "Nothing more. And nothing less."

"My father died in an accident, I..." Roland began to explain in despair.

The magician placed his hand on the boy's shoulder. Roland felt the metallic touch of his fingers.

"Half a minute, boy. It's a bit late for family stories."

The waves were now crashing against the deck of the bridge. Roland threw a last beseeching look at the magician. Cain knelt in front of him and smiled.

"Shall we make a deal, Jacob?" he whispered.

Tears sprang from Roland's eyes and he slowly nodded.

"Good, good, Jacob," murmured Cain. "Welcome home...."

The magician stood up and pointed toward one of the corridors that led from the bridge.

"The last door down that corridor. But here's a piece of advice. By the time you manage to open it we'll all be under water and your friend won't have enough air to breathe. You're a good diver, Jacob. You'll know what to do. Remember our pact...."

Cain smiled one last time and, wrapping himself in his cloak, disappeared into the night. Invisible feet echoed across the bridge, leaving behind footprints of molten

metal. The boy stood where he was for an instant, paralyzed, trying to recover his breath, until the ship gave
another jolt, pushing him against the frozen wheel of the
helm. Water had started to flood the bridge.

Roland rushed down the corridor the magician had
pointed out. Water was now pouring through the deck
hatches, inundating the corridor as the *Orpheus* gradually sank into the sea. Roland banged against the cabin
door with his fist.

"Alicia!" he shouted, although he was aware that she
could barely hear him. "It's Roland. Hold your breath!
I'm going to get you out of there!"

Roland grabbed the wheel that opened the cabin door
and struggled to turn it, hurting his hands as he did so.
The freezing water was already up to his waist and kept
on rising. The wheel only yielded a centimeter or so.
Roland took a deep breath and tried again. This time it
slowly rotated. The water was now over Roland's head.

When the door finally opened, Roland swam into the
murky cabin, groping around blindly for Alicia. For a
terrible moment he thought the magician had tricked him
and there was nobody there. He opened his eyes under
the water, battling against a stinging sensation, and tried
to see through the darkness. At last, his hands touched
a torn piece of Alicia's dress—she was still there, struggling between panic and suffocation. He hugged her and

tried to calm her, but in the dark she didn't know who or what had grabbed her. Aware that he had only a few seconds left, Roland put his hands around her shoulders and pulled her out into the corridor. The ship was still plunging toward the ocean bed. Alicia wrestled with Roland as he dragged her through the corridor toward the bridge, through the debris floating up from the depths of the *Orpheus*. He knew they couldn't get out of the ship until the hull had touched the bottom of the sea—if they tried before then, the pressure would only pull them back down—yet he was aware that at least thirty seconds had elapsed since Alicia had taken her last breath: By this time and in her state of panic, she had probably started to inhale water. If so, the ascent to the surface would mean certain death for her. Cain had planned this game with great care.

As they waited, it seemed as though the ship would never touch the bottom, and when the impact finally came, part of the ceiling in the bridge collapsed on top of them. A terrible pain shot up Roland's leg, and he realized that a piece of metal had trapped one of his ankles. Meanwhile, the glow of the *Orpheus* was slowly fading in the depths of the ocean.

Roland fought against the agonizing pain, searching for Alicia's face in the dark. Her eyes were open but she was struggling not to take in water. She couldn't hold her breath for another moment, and the last bubbles of air escaped from her lips like pearls carrying away the final moments of a life.

Roland held her face and tried to get Alicia to look at him. Their eyes locked and she understood immediately what he was proposing. Alicia shook her head, attempting to push Roland away from her. He pointed at his ankle, trapped under the metal beams from the ceiling. Alicia swam down through the icy water and tried to free him. They looked at one another in despair. Nothing and nobody would be able to move the tons of steel that were pinning Roland down. Alicia swam back to him and hugged him, aware that she was beginning to lose consciousness through lack of air. Without waiting another moment, Roland cupped Alicia's face with his hands and, placing his lips on hers, he breathed out the air he had kept for her, just as Cain had predicted he would. Alicia held Roland's hands tight and joined him in a lifesaving kiss.

Roland gave her one last, desperate look of farewell, then pushed her out of the bridge. Slowly, Alicia began her ascent. As she neared the surface, she kept her eyes fixed on Roland, his outline slowly fading in the murky shadows at the bottom of the sea. That was the last time Alicia saw Roland.

Seconds later, the girl emerged in the middle of the bay

and saw that the storm was gradually receding, taking with it all the hopes she had had for the future.

◆ ◆ ◆

When Max saw Alicia's face at the surface, he threw himself into the water and swam frantically toward her. His sister could barely stay afloat and was stammering incomprehensible words, coughing violently and spitting out the water she had swallowed on her way up. Max put his arms around her and swam with her until he was able to touch the stones with his feet, a few meters from the shore. The lighthouse keeper was waiting on the beach and rushed to help them. Together he and Max got Alicia out of the water and laid her down on her back. Victor Kray tried to take her pulse, but Max gently removed the old man's trembling hand.

"She's alive, Mr. Kray," Max explained, stroking his sister's forehead. "She's alive."

The old man nodded and left Alicia in Max's care. Stumbling like a soldier after a long battle, Victor Kray wandered down to the shore and waded into the water.

"Where's my Roland?" the old man moaned. "Where's my grandson?"

Max looked at him but could not find the words. He could see the soul of the poor man slipping away, and with it the strength that had sustained him all those years up in the lighthouse.

"He won't be coming back, Mr. Kray," Max replied eventually, his eyes brimming with tears. "Roland won't be coming back."

The lighthouse keeper looked at Max as if he didn't understand what he was saying. Then he nodded his head but turned his eyes seaward, still expecting his grandson to emerge and come back to him. The ocean gradually calmed and a garland of stars lit up over the horizon.

Roland never returned.

18

THE DAY AFTER THE STORM that ravaged the coast during the long night of June 23, 1943, Maximilian and Andrea Carver returned to the house by the beach with young Irina. She was no longer in danger, although it would be a few more weeks before she recovered completely from her injuries. The winds that had lashed the town until shortly before dawn had left a trail of fallen trees and electricity pylons, boats had been dragged in from the sea right up to the promenade, and there were many broken windows. Alicia and Max were sitting quietly on the porch. The moment Mr. Carver stepped out of the car that had brought them back from the hospital, he saw from their faces and their tattered clothing that something terrible had happened.

But before he could ask them anything, the expression on Max's face told him that all explanations, if there were to be any, would have to wait. Whatever it was that had happened, Maximilian Carver knew for certain, without any need for words or reasons, that the sadness of his two children signaled the end of a stage in their lives that would never return.

Maximilian Carver looked into Alicia's eyes before going into the house. She was staring absently at the horizon as if she thought it might hold the answer to all her questions—questions that neither he nor anyone else would be able to answer. Suddenly, and silently, he realized that his daughter had grown up and that one day, and it wouldn't be long, she would set off on a new path in search of her own answers.

♦ ♦ ♦

A cloud of steam engulfed the station. The last passengers were hurrying into the carriages of the train or bidding farewell to relatives and friends who had come with them as far as the platform. Max looked at the old station clock that had welcomed him to the town and noticed that, this time, its hands had stopped. The porter came over to Max and Victor Kray, his hand outstretched, hoping for a tip.

"Your suitcases are on the train, sir."

The old lighthouse keeper handed him a few coins and the porter walked away, counting them as he went. Max and Victor Kray exchanged a smile, as if they had found the incident amusing and this was only a routine farewell.

"Alicia wasn't able to come...." Max began.

"There's no need to explain. I understand," the lighthouse keeper said quickly. "Say good-bye to her from me. And take care of her."

"I will."

The stationmaster blew his whistle. The train was about to leave.

"Aren't you going to tell me where you're going?" asked Max, pointing at the train that was waiting on the track. Victor Kray smiled and offered his hand to the boy.

"Wherever I go," he replied, "I'll never be able to get away from here."

The whistle blew again. Victor Kray was the only person left to board. The ticket collector was waiting by the carriage door.

"I must go, Max," said the old man.

Victor Kray put his arms around him and Max hugged him tightly.

"By the way, I have something for you."

The lighthouse keeper handed over a small box. Something rattled inside it.

"Aren't you going to open it?"

"After you've gone," Max replied.

The lighthouse keeper shrugged his shoulders and walked over to the carriage. The ticket collector held out a hand to help him up. As he climbed the last step, Max suddenly ran toward him.

"Mr. Kray!"

The old man turned to look at him, an amused expression in his eyes.

"It was an honor to meet you, Mr. Kray," said Max.

Victor Kray smiled one last time and gently tapped his chest with his index finger.

"The name's Victor, Max. And the honor was all mine."

Slowly, the train began to pull away and soon its trail of steam was lost in the distance. Max stayed on the platform until he could no longer see the small dot on the horizon. Only then did he open the box the old man had given him and discover that it held a bunch of keys. Max smiled. They were the keys to the lighthouse.

EPILOGUE

THE LAST WEEKS OF SUMMER brought more news of the war whose days, it was said, were numbered. Maximilian Carver had opened his watchmaker's business in a small building near the market square, and soon there was not a single local who hadn't visited his shop of marvels. Irina had completely recovered and seemed to remember nothing about her accident on the staircase. She and her mother took long walks along the beach, looking for seashells and small fossils with which they had started a collection that promised to be the envy of Irina's new school friends that coming autumn.

Loyal to the old keeper's legacy, Max cycled every

afternoon to the lighthouse and lit the lantern so that its beam could guide ships safely until the following morning. He climbed up the tower and from there he gazed out at the ocean, just as Victor Kray had done for most of his life.

On one of these afternoons, Max realized that his sister Alicia returned regularly to the beach where Roland's hut stood. She went alone and sat by the water's edge, her eyes lost in the sea, letting the hours pass by in silence. They no longer spoke the way they had during the days they had shared with Roland, and Alicia never mentioned what had happened that night in the bay. Max had respected her silence from the first moment. When the last days of September arrived, announcing the arrival of the autumn, the memory of the Prince of Mist seemed to fade from his mind like a dream in the light of day.

Often, when Max watched his sister Alicia down on the beach, he remembered Roland's words when he had confessed his fear that if he was called up, this might be his last summer in the town. Now, although brother and sister barely spoke about it, Max knew that the memory of Roland, and of that summer in which they had discovered magic together, would stay with them, uniting them forever.

A Q&A with
CARLOS RUIZ ZAFÓN
and bestselling author
JAMES PATTERSON

JAMES PATTERSON: Your debut novel, *The Prince of Mist*, was originally published in Spanish in 1993. At that time, was it published and marketed at the young adult audience in Spain?

CARLOS RUIZ ZAFÓN: Yes, very much so.

◆ ◆ ◆

JP: So when you started writing the book, did you have that young adult audience in mind, or did you not really think about that until you'd finished crafting the tale?

CRZ: Absolutely. From the beginning I knew I was writing a story that was targeted mainly at readers twelve or thirteen years old. That was key in determining the overall design of the story, the register of the language, the narrative devices used, the characterization, etc. Having said that, I also wanted to write a book that would appeal to readers of all ages and that could be enjoyed as a relatively old-fashioned mystery-adventure tale with Victorian gothic overtones. In many ways I guess I was trying to write a book I would have loved to read when I was a teenager but could also enjoy later on.

◆ ◆ ◆

JP: I think the villain, Cain, in *The Prince of Mist* is particularly scary and compelling. How did you get the idea for his character, and for the story as a whole?

CRZ: I'd say Cain is a variation on the proverbial Faustian villain of many classic stories. I have always been intrigued by the role the devil plays as a literary character and a figure in myths, legends, and different religions. In some ways you could argue the devil is one of the most interesting literary characters ever created because it embodies many aspects of human nature we don't want to recognize in ourselves, or elements in nature we are in denial about. I think that kind of figure allows a storyteller many possibilities with symbols that can be shaped into the narrative. I see *The Prince of Mist* in part as a story about the end of childhood, the end of innocence, and the discovery of the dilemmas of adult life seen through the eyes of a kid. I think the plot came together from different ideas that had been in my mind and explored in a number of stories I had written before and never published.

◆ ◆ ◆

JP: I was struck by how incredibly cinematic your storytelling is. I'm a big fan of movies, and wonder if films influence your writing and scene structure at all. If so, are there any movies that you consider most inspiring to your aesthetic?

CRZ: Indeed, movies have played a huge part in shaping the way I tend to think of storytelling. In many ways, as a child, I would see films and literature as being parts of the same thing, pure storytelling. It was only later on, in my late teens and early twenties, that I began to differentiate and explore them separately. I believe that the basic grammar of movies is a by-product of nineteenth-century literature that has evolved into its own, quite sophisticated language and now can be deconstructed and employed to enrich the vast arsenal of narrative devices a novelist working in the twenty-first century has in his toolbox. Many movies have had a strong impact on me through the years. One of the most vivid memories of my childhood is watching Citizen Kane on my parents' old black-and-white TV set when I was not a day older than five. I was, and remain, mesmerized by that film. I could mention dozens of movies that have made a huge impact over the years on how I understand the mechanics and possibilities of storytelling. I would highlight a few: *Sunset Boulevard, Chinatown, The Godfather, Blade Runner, Schindler's*

List . . . and many, many others. I tend to think in images when it comes to building up a story, and I think imagery is a huge part of what I do as a writer to convey atmosphere, pace, and texture. Naturally, any kind of narrative language that uses images and sounds to communicate is of high interest to me, be it film, advertising, anime, comic books, any form of literary genre. . . . It is all language, one way or another. Codes, symbols, structure, logic . . . If it works, I'll try to dismantle it like a kid does with an old clock to figure out how it does what it does, and then reverse engineer it and use it for my own purposes in my work.

◆ ◆ ◆

JP: There are a lot of great scenes in *The Prince of Mist*—some of my favorites are those climactic scenes set on the ghost ship. Which scene is your favorite, if you have one? Which one was the most difficult to write?

CRZ: Probably the climax on the ghost ship arisen from the depths is my favorite part, too. I also like small brushstrokes here and there that provide an intimation of a character's inside process. The most difficult scenes to write tend to be those that involve many different elements and have to project a real-time illusion to the reader. The entire climactic sequence on the ship at the end is the kind of tricky thing that takes much fine-tuning to work.

◆ ◆ ◆

JP: The setting for the story is a coastal town in a time of war, but I noticed that it seems purposefully vague beyond that. Was that intentional, and if so, why?

CRZ: It is extremely vague, yes. Originally my idea was that the story was set in a small village on the south coast of England around 1942, somewhere between Brighton and Bournemouth. The big city the Carvers flee in the beginning would be London during the Blitz. Because I wanted to have readers project their own recollections of childhood and the memories of those long-lost summers in which we come of age into the story, I deliberately avoided pinpointing a specific place. The story could happen in a town on the coast of northern California or Oregon, or on the northern coast of Spain, or in the Mediterranean, or in many different places. It is not about a specific place. It is about the characters and what happens inside their minds during this magic, dark, and dangerous summer. So I made that choice, right or wrong.

◆ ◆ ◆

JP: I find that readers are often surprised by the amount of research authors sometimes do even for fiction and fantasy stories. Did you find yourself doing research to prepare to write *The Prince of Mist*?

CRZ: I think I am always doing research, piling up material on history, on architecture, on science . . . and then, eventually, I use it. I think you have to be careful with research in fiction. I believe the best way to use it is to learn a lot yourself about what you're going to write, and then don't really use more than 1 percent of all the research you've done, at least visibly. But you need to know all about it, because the effective way to use research in fiction is to internalize it and embed its essence in the narrative fabric of the tale. Information only works in fiction when it plays a dramatic role. Often you read novels in which the author includes much of the research he's done on a subject or a period or a place. None of that stuff sticks to the reader's brain unless it is instrumental in terms of story. It needs to work dramatically. It could work in a journalistic context or in a nonfiction book, but in literature you need to find a way to incorporate it in the texture, the aesthetics, and the fabric of the world you're building for the reader from a purely narrative point, never as window dressing or as a display of erudition. That way the readers absorb it without realizing they're doing it, and the function of research is achieved.

♦ ♦ ♦

JP: In my Maximum Ride, Daniel X, and Witch & Wizard series, the kid heroes face unimaginable threats against them, and usually triumph without adult intervention. Similarly in *The Prince of Mist*, Max, Alicia, and Roland are all teenagers confronted with extraordinary and dangerous situations, and don't immediately turn to adults for help. Was that a conscious decision, and if so, why?

CRZ: Yes, I think that is what most kids do in real life as well. Kids tend to inhabit their own universe, with their own logic.

When you have to face the dilemmas life presents you with, you have to do it on your own. That is part of growing up. You don't come of age holding hands with an adult. You do it on your own. *The Prince of Mist* tries to tell the story of how these three kids have to face a terrible evil and solve a diabolical mystery to survive. It is their story, and I wanted to tell it that way.

◆ ◆ ◆

JP: Reading *The Prince of Mist* has whetted my appetite for your next young adult book. Without giving too much away, can you tell us a bit about your next novel, *The Midnight Palace*, coming in May 2011?

CRZ: *The Midnight Palace* is a ghost story set in the city of Calcutta in the 1930s. It is a darker, more complex story than *The Prince of Mist*, although it shares the same "gothic" sensibility and involves young characters confronting a supernatural mystery. It is an adventure story that tries to take what *The Prince of Mist* is about and make it a more intense, more layered reading experience.

◆ ◆ ◆

JP: I know how much kids love series books. Are *The Prince of Mist* and *The Midnight Palace* connected in any way?

CRZ: I've always seen the three fist novels I published, from *The Prince of Mist* to a third one that will come after *The Midnight*

Palace called *September Lights*, as a trilogy of stories that share a common texture and aesthetic and explore similar themes. I believe each one takes the concept of this kind of story to a new level. I call these books The Trilogy of the Mist, and to me they are a world of stories with three doors of entry.

◆ ◆ ◆

JP: *The Midnight Palace* is set in Calcutta in the 1930s. What inspired you to set it there?

CRZ: At the time I was reading a lot of history, and I started to research this fascinating city almost by accident. I found out that the mere reality of Calcutta, and the first two hundred years of its history, were so filled with incredible, tragic, mysterious, and amazing stuff that it could provide an exciting arena to explore and build upon. The more I learned about the place, the more I realized it suited perfectly the kind of story I had in mind. I am interested in the notion of cities as characters, not mere backdrops. And Calcutta makes for a mesmerizing player.

◆ ◆ ◆

JP: *The Prince of Mist* was a bestselling book in Spain, but was only recently translated for an English-speaking audience. I wonder, what was the translation process like, and how were you involved in it? What was the experience like of reading your work in another language?

CRZ: I'm very lucky in that I've been working with the talented Lucia Graves on all the translations of my work into English, and by now I think we have developed what I feel is a tight operation. I am very involved in the translation process. Lucia works on a first draft, consulting with me as she sees fit, and then I take that and start reworking or rewriting and fine-tuning until I think what we have is as close to the original as possible. I think that we've managed to achieve that, and when I read my work in English I see very little difference from the original in terms of tone, pace, texture, flavor, and fluidity, and that most of the musicality of the language and the nuance of style and expression are there. I am obsessive about this and I am determined that the reader finds in English the very same book as in the original Spanish. On the rare occasions when something cannot be exactly translated, I will write something new from scratch in English that achieves exactly the same purpose. Literature is a hundred percent about language, so I make sure things are as tight as they need to be.

♦ ♦ ♦

JP: I aim to write stories that keep readers turning the pages and that continually evoke emotional responses. Without revealing too many secrets of your craft, what do you feel are the key ingredients of a spellbinding mystery?

CRZ: I think all stories, in a way, are mysteries. All stories are about exploration, revelation. . . . In practical terms I think mysteries are stories that are built on two sliding layers. One is about perception and illusion, the other about internal logistics of the timeline. As we advance, we remove the scaffolding of the first to reveal the second. Of course, this is a huge oversimplification. Readers tend to think they're excited by the story, but what they respond to, mainly, is the storytelling. It is not about the story; it is about how the story is told. Always. To me execution is everything. I firmly believe that literature is an art of results, not intentions. You only get as far as your craft and your technique allow you to. Mysteries are a perfect example of that. I think it is very interesting, and revelatory, to realize that when you look at the last thirty years of published fiction, much of the best writing and storytelling have been produced in or around that genre.

♦ ♦ ♦

JP: In writing for a younger audience, I especially love to create books that the whole family can enjoy together. What do you think are the biggest differences between writing for adult readers and for young adult readers, if any?

CRZ: Besides the obvious, or not-so-obvious, differences in the density of language, characterization, and tone, I believe the most important distinction lies in the need to provide YA fiction with an emotional foundation younger readers can relate to. I think kids who read are as smart and as sharp as most adults. If they are readers, they can understand intellectually any adult read, but what they may lack is the emotional baggage to relate to some of those stories because they are about something that has not happened yet in their lives. When you're in your teens, your emotional references are different from those in your twenties or thirties or forties or beyond. Hence, I think it is important to introduce in the story elements that they can relate to on a purely emotional level and not just understand intellectually. That said, I think it is very difficult to just pigeonhole young readers based purely on their age. To me, frankly, readers are readers, be they nine or ninety-nine years old. The distinctions and divisions of genre, labeling, and marketing can sometimes prove to be arbitrary and very hard to define. At the end of the day I just write for people who like to read, and I don't ask them for a driver's license to check their age. I aspire to write books that readers of many different kinds, conditions, and ages can enjoy and explore in their own way. I try to incorporate different levels of interpretation, and I do my best to build the books as places you can revisit at different times in your life and find something new and, hopefully, exciting.

◆ ◆ ◆

JP: Most of my series for younger readers include fantastical elements—like kids who can fly, aliens with superpowers, and kids who possess magic that can save the world from evil—because I love having the opportunity to let my imagination run wilder than it does in my adult work. Why are you drawn to writing about mystery and the supernatural?

CRZ: When you think of it, all fiction is fantasy. Realism is an aesthetic, a construct that belies the fact that we're all in the business of make-believe. I think fantasy just broadens the palette of colors and elements a storyteller can work with, and sometimes allows you as a writer to play with atavic and complex elements to elicit a response in the reader's mind. I do like to use supernatural elements in some books if I feel they are adequate and will allow me to more efficiently tell the story I'm trying to tell. On other occasions I refrain from that and stick to a more realistic tone, although I think that is just an illusion. I think that I am not prejudiced against the use of fantastical elements in fiction because as a reader, since childhood, I've read all sorts of genres and authors and never considered one above another just on the basis of labeling. To me it is about how well it is done, not about what you're trying to do.

◆ ◆ ◆

JP: I live in Florida and New York but do the bulk of my writing in Florida, where I spend most of the year. You divide your time between Barcelona, Spain, and Los Angeles, California. Are the two cities reflected in your work at all? Do you prefer to write in one or the other?

CRZ: I was born and raised in Barcelona, so the city is in many ways imprinted on me whether I like it or not. They say a writer's bank account is his childhood, and mine happened in Barcelona. On the other hand, I love America and find myself to be more productive there. I've written books on one side of the Atlantic, and books on the other side, and then books between one place and the other. I think the material I write in Barcelona tends to be darker, and what I write in America is more lyrical and hopeful. I wrote a book called *The Shadow of the Wind* entirely in Los Angeles, and to me it is very much a book about the years I've spent there, even if it is set in Barcelona. Then I wrote another novel, called *The Angel's Game*, mostly in Barcelona, and to me it is a book that captures much more honestly the true essence of the city. It is interesting how the places we live our lives in shape us and make us different people. I like to spend time in all sorts of places, be it Berlin, Paris, London, or anywhere in America. For some reason, I tend to be in a better, more positive mood in America. I don't know why. Maybe to me it is less haunted with memories. I think America, for a European at least, is more what you make of it than what it imposes on you. Perhaps for an American Europe would be like that as well? I don't know. I find Europe to be not so flexible. It is what it is, and rarely what you want to make of it. At least that is my own experience. I think possibly the places you choose affect you in a different ways from the places you've been given. On the other hand, for good or bad, I realize I am very much a product of old western Europe, and I like to spend time on both sides and try to enjoy the best of both worlds and, with any luck, reflect that in my work.

♦ ♦ ♦

JP: Young readers and aspiring writers often ask me about my writing process and my key strategy for consistently delivering good stories, and I always respond, "I outline. Outline, outline, outline." I know that not all writers use outlines, though. What's your writing process like? What's your favorite part of the process?

CRZ: Wise words. I do outline, outline, outline, but mostly I rewrite, rewrite, rewrite. And then rewrite it all again. To death. Until every single cog and screw in there is pushed so tight that if you tried to turn it a millimeter farther the whole thing would explode in your hands. I think that unless you're writing purely introspective and amorphous stuff, it is necessary that you know what you're doing. You need to know where you're going to get anywhere and to expect the reader to tag along with you. On the other hand, although I outline in what I call "layers"—that is, different kinds of outlines that are superimposed—I think it is also important to be flexible. Often, no matter how detailed and tight an outline might be, I find that once you're working on a specific problem, image, or beat, you realize there were levels of detail and complexity to it that you could not foresee when you were working on an overarching design. So you have to find new solutions to new problems, and that creates ripple effects in all directions, which force you to redesign and reinforce the whole thing again. To me a novel is a cathedral made of words. The most important aspects of it all are the architecture and engineering of the whole thing, and the essence of that, for me, is language. Style. So my favorite part in the process is after I've managed to get things right enough to do a final polish and drive it to the point where I think I cannot make it better. Not because it cannot be made better, but because I don't know how, and since I built the engine and know how it works, nobody else really can, either. That's when I think the book is finished, and then nobody touches a comma. I once heard an author say that he didn't enjoy writing, he enjoyed having written. I couldn't agree more. To me writing is hard work. I feel I'm squeezing my brain there in front of the blank page, and it is not always fun. But I enjoy the sense of having achieved what I set out to do.

◆ ◆ ◆

JP: Some books for kids that I admire are *The Invention of Hugo Cabret* and *The Hunger Games*. What are a few of your favorite books for young readers? What did you read when you were a teen? What do you read now for inspiration?

CRZ: I confess I have a relatively unorthodox view of what makes a young adult book. When I was a kid, I never read books because they were labeled one way or another. I just read what intrigued me. I used to read a lot of noir fiction, and science fiction and fantasy, but I also read Dickens, or Poe, or John Steinbeck, or Thomas Mann, or anything I found interesting. I would read every single Stephen King book I could find, and then I would read Raymond Chandler or Ross MacDonald, and then move on to William Faulkner (although very often I couldn't figure it out until years later) or anything that looked promising. And a lot of it looked very promising to me. I just read. My idea of a wonderful book for young readers is Harper Lee's *To Kill a Mockingbird*, for instance. There's a lot of terrific stuff out there for kids to enjoy and get excited about. I tend to read all sorts of things. I read a lot of nonfiction, mostly history. In fiction I read without prejudice. I try to ignore clichéd notions about what I should think and read dictated by what I call the gatekeepers of thought, and I make a point of constantly trying new things and new, or sometimes not-so-new, authors. Right now I am going through a feverish phase of reading the entire works of John LeCarre, and every day I am increasingly in awe of the man. Sentence by sentence, I doubt you could find a finer writer working in the last four decades. Pure magic. I just like to discover the beauty of great writing wherever it is—a genre novel, a classic, an obscure title, or a bestselling mystery on the *New York Times* list. I don't care what the label on it is or what I am told I should think of it. I care about what it is inside. I'll decide what I think of it by myself.

◆ ◆ ◆

JP: Some people are surprised to discover that I was out of school before I really discovered the joy of reading and writing. Like a lot of kids, I was kind of put off in school, where a lot of boring books were assigned. Were you a big reader as a child? Did you always want to be a writer? If not, what did you think you'd grow up to be, and how did you eventually end up choosing writing as a career?

CRZ: For some reason I always knew I wanted to be a writer. Or I should say I always knew I would be a writer because I had no other choice. I came like that out of the factory. I've been making up stories and telling them for as long as I can remember.

It is what I do. I've just been trying to get better at it ever since. I read a lot as a kid, but rarely the books that were assigned to me. I read what I wanted, not what others wanted me to read. I think this has changed a lot since my days as a schoolkid, and in modern schools teachers are allowed much more freedom to choose books that will prove exciting and will motivate the kids to read more, rather than dull medieval relics of arcane language that no twelve-year-old in the history of the world would ever get through, even at gunpoint.

I guess if I weren't a writer I would be a musician. Music is what I love most in the world, more even than books. One of the great regrets of my life is that I never had the chance to get a musical education. I did teach myself to play the piano, and I would study on my own dense and not exactly page-turning tomes on harmony, composition, counterpoint, and orchestration, just to try to figure it all out. Music is probably the biggest influence on my writing, strange as it may seem.

♦ ♦ ♦

JP: Now I get to ask you the question that I always get asked: Can you offer any advice for young aspiring authors?

CRZ: Read. Read. Read. I would say that advice is good for any young person aspiring to become anything—an author, an engineer, or just any human being able to live more and live better. In the case of aspiring writers, I think that to become a writer, first you have to be a reader. You need to read widely, without prejudice, and learn from what you read. Understand how the language is composed and bent, how an author builds characters, stages a scene, or paints an image. And then, after you've read a lot, you need to write. A lot. You need to get out there and work hard, and fill hundreds or thousands of pages maybe nobody will ever read until you're able to write one that merits other people's time and attention. You have to try to be the very best you can be, no matter what it is you want to do in life. If you want to be an author, you better work very hard, because it is a tough game and it is not easy to make a living as a writer at all. When one is young one doesn't realize how short life is. But it is. Give it all you've got, and then some.

JAMES PATTERSON was selected by teens across America as the Children's Choice Book Awards Author of the Year in 2010. He is the internationally bestselling author of the highly praised Maximum Ride novels, the Witch & Wizard series, the Daniel X series, *Med Head*, and the detective series featuring Alex Cross and the Women's Murder Club. His books have sold more than 205 million copies worldwide, making him one of the bestselling authors of all time. He lives in Florida.

AN ANCIENT TERROR
LURKS IN THE SHADOWS....

"Zafón is a master storyteller." —*VOYA* (starred review)

THE
MIDNIGHT
PALACE

Author of the *New York Times* bestseller *The Prince of Mist*

CARLOS RUIZ ZAFÓN

TURN THE PAGE FOR A SNEAK PEEK
AT CARLOS RUIZ ZAFÓN'S NEXT
CHILLING TALE

COMING MAY 2011

THE RETURN OF DARKNESS
CALCUTTA, MAY 1916

SHORTLY AFTER MIDNIGHT, a boat emerged out of the mist that rose like a fetid curse from the surface of the Hooghly River. The faint glow of a flickering lantern attached to the mast revealed the figure of a man wrapped in a cape, rowing with difficulty toward the distant shore. Farther to the east, under a blanket of leaden clouds, the outline of Fort William in the Maidan—a sort of Hyde Park carved out of tropical jungle—stood out against an endless expanse of streetlamps and bonfires that spread as far as the eye could see. Calcutta.

The man stopped for a few moments to recover his breath and look back at the silhouette of Jheeter's Gate

Station, rising from the shadows on the opposite bank. The farther he went, the more the station made of glass and steel seemed to melt into the city—a jungle of marble mausoleums blackened by decades of neglect; naked walls once coated in ocher, blue, and gold, their colors peeled away by the fury of the monsoon, leaving them blurred and faded, like watercolors dissolving in a pond.

Only the certainty that he had just a few hours to live—perhaps only a few minutes—kept him going, leaving behind in that ill-fated place the woman he had sworn to protect. As Lieutenant Peake made his last journey to Calcutta, aboard an old rowboat, the rain that had arrived in the early hours of darkness was washing away every last second of his life.

While he struggled to row the boat toward the shore, the lieutenant could hear the crying of the two babies hidden inside the bilge. Peake turned his head and noticed the lights of the other boat twinkling only a hundred meters behind him. He pictured the smile of his pursuer, savoring the hunt for his prey. Relentless.

Ignoring the children's tears of hunger and cold, he applied his remaining strength to steering the boat toward the threshold that led into the ghostly labyrinth of streets. Two hundred years had been enough to transform the thick jungle growing around Kalighat into a city even God did not dare enter.

In a matter of minutes the storm looming over the city had unleashed its fury. By mid-April and well into the month of June, the city withered in the clutches of the so-called Indian summer, with temperatures reaching up to one hundred ten degrees and a level of humidity close to saturation. But with the arrival of violent electric storms that turned the sky into a battle scene, thermometers could plunge thirty degrees in a few moments.

The curtain of rain hid the unsteady jetties of rotten wood that dangled over the water's edge, but Peake didn't stop until he felt the hull hitting the planks of the fishermen's dock. Only then did he thrust the anchoring pole into the muddy riverbed and rush to extract the children, who lay wrapped in a blanket. As he took them in his arms, the crying of the babies permeated the night like a trail of blood calling out to the predator. Pressing the bundle against his chest, Peake jumped ashore.

As the rain pelted down, he saw the other boat approaching the riverbank, slowly, like a funeral barge. Gripped with fear, Peake ran toward the streets bordering the southern edge of the Maidan, a district known by its privileged residents—mostly British and Europeans—as the White Town.

He clung to one remaining hope of being able to save the children, but he was still far from the heart of North Calcutta and Aryami Bose's house. The old lady was the only person who could help him now. Peake stopped for a moment and scanned the gloomy expanse of the Maidan, searching for the distant glow of the streetlamps that flickered in the northern part of the city. The dark streets, cloaked by the storm, would be his safest hiding place. Holding the children tight, Lieutenant Peake set off again, heading east, hoping to find cover in the shadows cast by the palatial buildings of the city center.

Moments later, the black barge that had been pursuing him came to a halt by the dock. Three men jumped ashore and moored the vessel. The small cabin door slowly opened and a dark figure, wrapped in a black cloak, crossed the gangplank the men had laid from the jetty, ignoring the rain. Once ashore, the figure stretched out a black-gloved hand and, pointing to the place where Peake had disappeared, gave a sinister smile.

◆ ◆ ◆

The winding road that cut across the Maidan, rounding the fortress, had turned into a swamp under the pounding rain. Peake vaguely remembered having crossed that part of the city in the days when he was serving under Colonel Llewelyn. But that had been in broad daylight, on horseback, and surrounded by an armed cavalry regiment. Ironically, fate now took him along the same stretch of open fields that had been leveled by Lord Clive in 1758 so that the cannons of Fort William could enjoy a clear line of fire in all directions. Only this time he was the target.

Lieutenant Peake ran toward a cluster of trees, sensing the furtive gaze of those hidden in the dark, the nocturnal inhabitants of the Maidan. He knew that nobody here would try to waylay him and snatch his cape or take the children who were crying in his arms. The invisible presences could smell death clinging to his heels, and not a soul would dare come between him and his pursuer.

Peake jumped over the railing separating the Maidan from Chowringhee Road and entered the main artery of Calcutta. The majestic avenue had been built on top of the old path that, only three hundred years earlier, had crossed the Bengali jungle southward, leading to the temple of Kali, the Kalighat, which gave the city its name.

Because of the rain, the swarm of people who usually prowled the area at night had retreated and the city looked like a large, empty bazaar. Peake knew that the veil of rain that blurred his vision, but also shrouded him, could vanish as instantly as it had appeared. The storms that entered the Ganges Delta from the ocean quickly traveled north or west after discharging their deluge on the Bengali Peninsula, leaving behind a trail of mist and flooded streets where children played in filthy puddles and carts ran aground in the mud like drifting ships.

The lieutenant ran along Chowringhee Road until he felt the muscles of his legs giving way and he was barely able to support the weight of the babies. He could see the lights of the northern district, but he knew he would not be able to keep up this pace much longer, and Aryami Bose's house was still a good distance away. He had to make a stop.

He paused to get his breath back under the staircase of an old textile warehouse, the walls of which were covered in official notices announcing its imminent demolition. He vaguely recalled having inspected the place years earlier, after some rich merchant had reported that it concealed a notorious opium den.

Now, dirty water poured down the crumbling stairs like dark blood gushing from a wound. The place seemed deserted. Lieutenant Peake lifted the children close to his face and looked into their eyes; the two babies were no longer crying, but they were trembling from the cold, and the blanket that covered them was almost completely soaked. Peake held their tiny hands in his, hoping to give them some warmth as he peeped through the cracks in the staircase, keeping an eye on the streets leading off the Maidan. He couldn't remember how many assassins his pursuer had recruited, but he knew that there were only two bullets left in his revolver, two bullets he would have to use with all the cunning he could muster—he had fired the rest of his ammunition in the tunnels of the railway station. Peake wrapped the children in the drier part of the blanket and left them lying on a bit of dry floor he spied in a hollow in the warehouse wall.

He pulled out his revolver, slowly peering around the side of the stairs. He strained his eyes and recognized the line of distant lights on the other side of the Hooghly River. The sound of hurried footsteps startled him, and he moved back into the shadows.

Three men emerged from the darkness of the Maidan, the blades of their knives shining in the gloom. Peake rushed to gather the children in his arms once again and took a deep breath, aware that if he were to flee at that moment, the men would fall on him like a pack of wolves.

The lieutenant stood motionless against the wall, watching his pursuers as they stopped to search for his trail. The assassins exchanged a few mumbled words, and then one signaled to the other two that they should separate. Peake shuddered as he realized that the one who had given the order was now approaching the staircase; for a split second he thought that the smell of his fear alone would lead the killer to his hiding place.

Desperately, he scanned the wall below the staircase in

search of some gap through which he could escape. He kneeled down by the hollow where he had left the babies a few seconds earlier and tried to dislodge the planks, which were loose and softened by the dampness. The rotten wood yielded easily, and Peake felt a breath of noxious air escaping from the dilapidated building. He turned his head and saw the murderer standing only twenty meters away, at the foot of the staircase, brandishing his knife.

He wrapped the babies in his own cape for protection and crawled through the hole and into the warehouse. A sharp pain, just above his knee, suddenly paralyzed his right leg. Peake patted the leg with trembling hands and found a rusty nail sunk into his flesh. Stifling a scream, he grabbed the tip of the cold metal and pulled hard. He felt the skin tearing, and warm blood trickled through his fingers. A wave of nausea and pain clouded his vision. Gasping, he gathered the babies and struggled to his feet. An eerie passageway with hundreds of empty shelves spread before him. Without a moment's hesitation, Peake ran toward the other end of the warehouse, the wounded structure creaking in the storm.

◆ ◆ ◆

When Peake reemerged into the night after running hundreds of meters through the bowels of the ruined building, he discovered he was only a stone's throw from the Tiretta Bazar, one of the commercial centers of North Calcutta. He thanked his lucky stars and set off toward the jumble of narrow streets, heading straight for the house of Aryami Bose.

It took him ten minutes to reach the home of the last woman in the Bose family line. Aryami lived alone in a sprawling house built in the Bengali style that rose amid the thick, wild vegetation that had invaded the courtyard over the years, making the place look abandoned. Yet no inhabitant of North Calcutta—an area also known as the Black Town—would have dared go beyond that courtyard and enter the estate of Aryami Bose. Those who knew her loved and respected her as much as they feared her. And there wasn't a soul in the streets of North Calcutta who hadn't heard of Aryami Bose and her ancestry. For the people of the area she was like a spirit: an invisible and powerful presence.

Peake ran to the spear-headed gates, through the over-grown courtyard, and up the cracked marble staircase that led to the front door. Holding both babies under one arm, he banged repeatedly with his fist, hoping he would be heard through the storm.

The lieutenant continued to pound on the door for a good five minutes, his eyes fixed on the deserted streets behind him, fearing he would catch sight of his pursuers at any moment. When the door finally yielded, Peake turned around and was blinded by the light of a candle. A voice he hadn't heard in five years whispered his name. He shaded his eyes with one hand and recognized the inscrutable face of Aryami Bose.

The woman read his expression and gazed down at the children, a shadow of pain passing over her face.

"She's dead, Aryami," murmured Peake. "She was already dead when I found her."

Aryami closed her eyes and breathed deeply. Peake saw that the news cut deep into the lady's heart, confirming her worst suspicions.

"Come in," she said at last, letting him pass and closing the door behind him.

Peake hurried over to a table, where he laid down the babies and removed their wet clothes. Without saying a word, Aryami fetched some dry strips of cloth and wrapped the children in them while Peake stoked the fire.

"I'm being followed, Aryami," said Peake. "I can't stay here."

"You're wounded," said the woman, pointing to the gash from the nail.

"Just a scratch," Peake lied. "It doesn't hurt."

Aryami moved closer to him and stretched out her hand to stroke his face.

"You always loved her..."

Peake turned his head away and didn't reply.

"They could have been your children," said Aryami. "They might have had better luck."

"I must go, Aryami," the lieutenant insisted. "If I stay here they'll find me. They won't give up."

They exchanged a defeated look, both aware of the fate that awaited Peake as soon as he returned to the streets. Aryami took his hands in hers and pressed them tightly.

"I was never good to you," she said. "I feared for my daughter, for the life she might have had with a British officer. But I was wrong. I suppose you'll never forgive me."

"It doesn't matter anymore," replied Peake. "I *must* go. Right now."

He took one last look at the babies, who had settled quietly by the fire. They looked at him, their eyes bright. At last they were safe. The lieutenant walked to the door and took a deep breath. Exhaustion and the throbbing pain in his leg overwhelmed him after the few moments of rest. He had used the last reserves of his strength to bring the infants to this place, and now he wondered how he was going to face the inevitable. Outside, the rain was still lashing down, but there was no sign of his pursuer or his henchmen.

"Michael..." said Aryami behind him.

The young man stopped but didn't turn around.

"She knew," Aryami lied. "She knew from the start and I'm sure that, in some way, she felt the same for you. It was my fault. Don't hold it against her."

Peake replied with a nod and closed the door behind him. For a few seconds he stood there, in the rain, finally at peace with himself; then he set off to meet his pursuers. After retracing his steps back to the abandoned warehouse, he entered the dark building once more in search of a hiding place.

As he crouched in the shadows, weariness and pain fused slowly into a drunken sense of calm, and his lips betrayed a faint smile. He no longer had any reason, or hope, to go on living.